Longing for More

ENCHANTED MOUNTAINS series

~

Eleanor Romany

Longing for More
Book One of the *Enchanted Mountains* series
Cover designed using Canva
Published by Eleanor Romany via Kindle Direct Publishing
ISBN: 9798999679673
First Edition
Published in the
United States of America
10 9 8 7 6 5 4 3 2 1

This book is dedicated to Tiffany,
my friend of nearly 25 years.
She is one of the strongest, funniest,
and smartest women I've ever known.

She is also one of the most insatiable readers
you'll ever meet—always starting
or finishing a book, getting ready to find one,
or waiting to recommend one to you.

For that and so many other reasons,
Tiffany, this one is for you.

Longing for More

ENCHANTED MOUNTAINS series

Chapter 1

Mariah Rivera pulled open the heavy wooden doors of Twin Pines Lodge and walked quickly inside, her heart racing. She looked at her watch; it was two fifty-five p.m. She had exactly five minutes until the rush of the week's guests descended upon the front desk to check into their cabins at Twin Pines State Park.

"Cutting it close again, I see!" a familiar voice rang out.

Mariah smiled at Jeffrey Long, who was sitting behind the desk. They had both worked at the park for many years and had recently grown closer as friends.

"You know me, I lose track of time staring out at the lake on my breaks." She smoothed down her light brown hair and adjusted her hunter green polo that was the park employee uniform.

Even though she had worked there for years and had visited the park more times than she could count growing up nearby, Mariah was forever mesmerized by the towering pine trees that surrounded the glittering lake. For more than 100 years, Twin Pines State Park's magnificent natural sanctuary had beckoned visitors with its scenic beauty and deep sense of tranquility. Families returned year after year, seeking adventure, relaxation, and a deeper connection with nature.

And then there was Mariah, who sought it out every day, not just once a year. The park, nestled deep in the Enchanted Mountains, had become her sanctuary, a place where she found solace and freedom.

Those majestic evergreens were dependable and strong, something she lacked in her life. Especially when it came to the shallow dating pool she'd been swimming in the past several years.

She walked behind the registration desk and took her seat on the stool next to Jeffrey. "How do I look?"

"Like you just ran a mile," he laughed.

The front lobby was already filling up with guests waiting to check in. Visitors liked to get inside their cabins as soon as they could and begin their vacations. Cabin keys, attached to plastic burgundy fobs with the trail name and number written on it, were badges of pride that guests carried around all week.

The line that afternoon snaked the length of the registration desk and around the corner in front of the gift shop. As soon as her watch hit three o'clock, Mariah looked up at the first guest in line.

"Welcome to Twin Pines State Park, how may I help you?"

Forty minutes later, the line disappeared and the lobby was filled with kids running toward the museum on one end and parents holding T-shirts and magnets they'd just bought from the gift shop at the other end.

"Wow, that was nuts," Jeffrey said under his breath as he pushed a New York State fishing license across the desk to a woman and thanked her for visiting. He stood up from his stool and stretched. "It'll be nice to have a quick break."

Mariah was thinking the same thing. But just as she was about to sneak away, the front doors burst open and a big family walked in, talking and laughing.

"Back to work!" Jeffrey sighed. Mariah sat back down on her stool, too, watching the family approach Jeffrey. Thinking she had lucked out, she was startled when a man suddenly appeared before her.

He had an almost childlike enthusiasm radiating from his face as he smiled quickly at Mariah and then looked around the lobby, taking it all in.

"Hi there, welcome to Twin Pines State Park!" Mariah stammered, caught off guard by his sudden presence and his piercing green eyes. "How can I assist you today?"

Mariah could tell he was an athlete: his body was slender and lean beneath his simple yet expensive clothing. Even though his face was covered in a thin, dark brown beard, his strong jawline was evident. He looked like what locals called a 'city boy,' but from the expression on his face, she could tell this wasn't his first time at Twin Pines Lodge.

It was the most handsome face Mariah had ever seen. She watched him, mesmerized. Suddenly, he focused his attention directly on her as if he was just noticing her sitting there.

"I'd like to check into my cabin! My name is Luke Anderson, reservation should be under Paul Anderson. I've been vacationing here with my family all my life." He gestured toward a couple standing nearby that was gathering brochures from a display case. "But it's been five years since I last visited." His words came out so fast he almost tripped over them.

Mariah wasn't surprised. Families who had been coming to Twin Pines for years loved to share their family's history with the park.

"That's wonderful. We're thrilled to have you return after such a long time." Mariah hoped her voice wasn't as high-pitched as it sounded to her. "Let me find the reservation in our system."

Moments later, she found what she was searching for and looked up. "East Meadows Trail, cabin fifteen, right?"

Luke nodded, his excitement growing. "Yes, that's the one! It's always been my family's favorite cabin. I have so many memories from this place." He looked around the lobby, smiling softly, off again in his own little world.

Mariah reached behind her and grabbed a key hanging on a thumbtack stuck in the bulletin board. She slid it across the counter, and as he picked it up, Luke's fingertips brushed the top of her hand.

And they lingered. Mariah's face felt hot, and the room seemed smaller. She could feel her polo soaking up the sweat suddenly rolling down her back. She jerked her hand off the counter and placed it in her lap.

Did I just imagine that? she wondered. She was too nervous to look up. When she finally did, after what felt like five minutes, Luke was looking at her expectantly.

"Is that for me?" He pointed to a glossy brochure Mariah was holding.

"Oh, yes, here, it's a..." Mariah's thoughts trailed off as she handed him a park map, crinkled and bent where she had gripped it so tightly. She quickly gathered herself.

"I'm sure you'll find everything just as you remember it. Quite frankly, not much has changed since you were last here. Or since you were a kid!"

Luke laughed loudly... too loudly for Mariah's lame joke.

She cleared her throat. "If you need anything, let us know. If this desk isn't open, the night attendant can help."

"Thank you..." he paused. "What's your name?"

Mariah looked down at her nametag, as if she had to check. Her face flushed as Luke laughed.

"I see. Thank you so much, Mariah. It's nice to be back."

~

"What on Earth is wrong with you?" Jeffrey watched Luke walk out of the lodge. "Do you know him?"

Mariah felt her heart beating fast. She twisted the lid off her water bottle and chugged.

"Okay, wow, I'll wait until you're finished."

Mariah laughed as she wiped drops of water off her lips and shook her head.

"No, I don't know him, but..."

"But what?"

"No, never mind." Her face flushed just thinking about telling him. Her damp shirt clung to the small of her back.

"Oh no, you have to spill it." Jeffrey reached behind them and flipped the *We're Open* sign to *Be Back Soon* and moved the little clock hands to ten minutes in the future. "Let's go upstairs."

Mariah sighed, still feeling flustered, but followed him past the gift shop and up the wooden, creaky stairs to Twin Pines Restaurant. The wood-paneled dining room was filled with bright afternoon sunlight, and the tables were covered with green-and-white checkered tablecloths, shiny from being wiped down. The restaurant was empty while staff members bustled around, cleaning in between lunch and dinner.

Jeffrey grabbed a table overlooking the lake and gestured for Mariah to sit down.

"Okay, damsel in distress. Spill it."

Mariah inhaled, knowing that her friend was going to think she was being ridiculous. She put her arms on the table and clasped her hands together.

"There's something about that guy, the one I checked in. When I handed him his cabin key, I swear he...he..."

Jeffrey stared at her, his mouth slightly open and his eyes wide.

"He was the hottest man to ever come to the park?" Jeffrey finally said, breaking the silence.

Mariah laughed. "Other than that. He…"

"Uh huh…"

"I think he grabbed my hand and…and he held onto it!"

Two seconds of silence passed before Jeffrey burst into the loudest laugh Mariah had ever heard. She looked around the room, not wanting to draw attention.

"Are you sure?" he asked incredulously. "Are you sure he would do something so… scandalous?!"

Mariah shook her head and looked out the window, her cheeks burning with embarrassment. She took in the rolling hills of pine trees, the canoes on the glistening water, and the teenagers speeding on their bikes along the path around the lake.

"We need to get back downstairs." Before Jeffrey could protest, she stood up, pushed in the heavy wooden chair, and left the restaurant.

~

With his cabin key in hand, Luke slid into his Audi A5 and slowly backed out of his parking spot, his parents falling in behind. Keeping an eye out for people and animals crossing the road, he carefully maneuvered around the back of the lodge and down the hill toward the road.

He counted the seconds until the view of the lake appeared between the evergreens. As soon as he saw it, he felt something in the pit of his stomach. He wasn't sure if it was excitement, nervousness, relief, or some combination of all three.

All he knew was that he felt different than he had when he left his apartment in New York City that morning. Like he was a different person.

His family had vacationed at Twin Pines for as long as he could remember. His grandparents had started the tradition and now his parents kept it alive, having invited him for the past several years even though he turned them down each time.

It wasn't that he hadn't wanted to go. He just found he always had more pressing matters.

Luke had quickly risen through the ranks at Mediaverse Global from Account Executive to VP of Global Partnerships, becoming the company's youngest vice president at the age of thirty-one. His ascent had been dizzying. Almost as dizzying as the increasing salary and perks that came with it… and the dating escapades that came with that.

He rarely left New York City for pleasure, instead traveling to places like Shanghai or Sydney monthly to negotiate and finalize major corporate partnerships and alliances for his company.

So when he actually accepted his parents' invitation at the last minute to spend a week at Twin Pines, it was a shock to all of them. Deep down, though, Luke knew a trip to his childhood sanctuary was exactly what he needed.

The other thing Luke knew he needed, as he slowly drove toward East Meadows Trail, was to see the woman from the lodge again.

He couldn't get the image of her out of his mind. In the bright warmth of the afternoon sun, Mariah had looked like she was glowing. Her long brown hair cascaded in loose waves, framing her bright, olive-toned face. Luke had been so distracted that he knew he'd let his hand linger a little too long as he grabbed the cabin key. He hoped he hadn't come off like a weirdo, and his cheeks burned crimson at the thought.

And even though Mariah was in her work uniform and half hidden behind the desk, Luke could tell by the way her shirt hugged her and the grace of her slender neck that she was one of the prettiest women he'd ever seen.

He cleared his throat. This wasn't the time for those kinds of thoughts, as he looked in his rearview mirror at his parents' SUV. He put on his turn signal and made a right onto East Meadows Trail, wincing a little as his sports car dragged over the gravel up the hill to cabin fifteen.

~

"That should be the last of it!" Luke said as he shoved a duffel bag onto the top bunk. Even though it was a delightful seventy-two degrees outside, sweat rolled down his forehead from unpacking their cars. He reached into his parents' cooler.

"Help yourself, son," Luke's dad, Paul, said. "There's plenty in there."

Luke cracked open a can of beer and handed it to his dad before doing the same for himself.

"We're so happy to have you here," Paul said. "Your mom especially, this is such a treat."

Luke smiled and placed a hand on his dad's shoulder.

"I'm happy to be here. It's been too long. These old cabins sure haven't changed, have they?"

Mariah had been right about that: so far, nothing had truly changed since he was a kid. The one-room cabin, with its small kitchen area, two sets of bunk beds, and heavy wooden picnic table and benches, somehow smelled musty and fresh at the same time.

Since his decision to come to the park was so last minute, he had decided to share his parents' cabin. He'd barely had time to pack, figuring whatever he didn't bring he could pick up in town.

The door opened with that familiar creak Luke knew well and gently slammed as his mother, Martha, came back inside.

"The cars are finally unpacked, thanks to you!" she said, smiling at her son. "Let's sit down and rest for a minute. I see you both have drinks, I'm going to get one, too."

Martha poured chilled white wine into a plastic cup and brought it over to the picnic table where Luke and Paul were sitting.

"Cheers to a wonderful vacation," she said, holding her cup up high.

"Cheers!" the men said in unison, clinking their cans together.

Luke smiled to himself, as the warmth of the wilderness and the drink flowed over his body. It really did feel good to be back here, with his family and in this cabin full of so many memories. Then his mom's voice broke his thoughts.

"How's New York? Is the crime still out of control?"

"Mom, it's not bad." She always began their catchups with this question. "Not as bad as any other big city. Besides, my apartment is in a good neighborhood. You've been there."

"I don't know why you still rent that apartment when you can afford to buy one," Martha said, the wine seeming to make her more opinionated very quickly.

"Buying a home is a big decision. It's not just about how much money I'm making, Mom."

"How much *are* you making now?" Martha tilted her head toward the front of the cabin where his car was parked.

Luke sighed softly. *That feeling of relaxation didn't last long,* he thought. He reached into the cooler and grabbed another beer.

"It was such a surprise when you called the other day. After five years, I told your dad that we might as well stop asking—"

"We were never going to stop asking you to join us here," Paul interrupted with a wink. "We know how busy that job keeps you and how important you are to the company. It looks like you're still doing well, yeah?"

Paul moved aside the thin white curtains to peek out the window at Luke's car. Its blue metallic paint sparkled in the sun despite all the bugs and dust.

"Yeah, still doing well, Dad. Can't complain." Luke's jaw clenched and his thick eyebrows knitted with tension. Only two hours at the park and he was already regretting not even trying to get his own cabin.

Eager to change the subject, he started to ask how his cousins were doing when his mom put down her drink and stood up.

"Before it gets too late, we need to run into town and buy some firewood. It's a good night for roasting marshmallows."

"Sounds good, I'll go with you," Paul said. "What about you, son?"

Luke felt a jolt of excitement at the idea of spending even a little bit of time by himself. "No, you two go, and I'll finish unpacking my things."

"We'll grab something for dinner while we're out," Paul added as he finished his beer.

Suddenly, Luke's mind was racing, and he felt his heart rate increase ever so slightly.

"Let's go to Twin Pines Restaurant for dinner," he offered. "It's been a long day for all of us. No one should have to cook."

"Oh, I don't mind," his mother began. "We can—"

Luke cut her off.

"Then it's settled, and it's my treat. You two better get back with the firewood soon. I'll meet you at the lodge." He quickly ushered them out of the cabin.

As soon as Paul and Martha's car disappeared, Luke felt more energy than he had all day. His shoulders relaxed, though he still felt that gnawing in the pit of his stomach.

The way he had it figured, he had about thirty minutes to run to the showers and wash away the stress of the day, change into something nice, but not *too* nice, and get back over to the lodge.

He had to see Mariah. He glanced down at the picnic table where he had thrown the crumpled map she had handed him.

Luke had to see her again to make sure the vision he had in his head was real... and that the exhaustion he felt from life or the magic of being back at the park hadn't caused him to make her up.

~

Later that evening, as Luke held the lodge door open for his parents, his heart pounded at the idea of locking eyes with Mariah. But when he stepped inside and his gaze fell where he'd seen her earlier, it was empty.

He approached the counter and noticed a note lying there: *For assistance, please speak with the night desk*, with an arrow pointing down to the other side of the lobby. He looked in that direction but only saw a young man with earbuds reading a magazine and bobbing his head to music.

Luke felt disappointed. But once they were seated in the restaurant, he felt himself begin to relax again. Twin Pines had that effect. It was hard to be disappointed surrounded by such regal nature. He looked out the window and smiled.

The sun bathed the sky in a symphony of warm and vibrant colors. The tranquil water of the lake reflected the hues, creating a mesmerizing mirror image that seemed to blend the boundaries between earth and sky.

He wondered if Mariah was enjoying it, too. He wondered where she was and if the shiny waves of her hair were pulled up in a ponytail or resting gently on her shoulders. He wondered if she was going crazy thinking about him as much as he was thinking about her.

Crazy, he suddenly thought. *That's the key word here.* He was acting like a school-age boy with a silly crush. *It didn't make any sense,* he thought to himself, almost shaking his head at the idea. He'd spent five minutes with her.

"This place has the best sunsets I've ever seen... and the best fish and chips!" Martha said as the waiter brought their food.

"Have you been to a Yankees game this summer?" Paul asked before taking a bite of his hamburger.

"Actually, yeah!" Luke said, thankful for the distraction from his own thoughts. "I caught one a few weeks ago. I'd just gotten back from a quick trip to Toronto and wanted to spend some time outdoors."

"Oh that's nice, dear," his mother said. "Did you go with your friends?"

Not exactly, Luke thought. He had gone with a woman named Katrina. They'd already been on one date: dinner at a five-star French restaurant in SoHo, then tickets to the philharmonic. It had gone well, but then as usual, Luke's job took over, and he didn't call Katrina for three weeks. When he got back from Toronto, he thought the baseball game might be a good way to start over with her.

But when Katrina shook his hand after the game and thanked him for the "interesting evening," he knew he'd never see her again. He realized too late that going from French cuisine to sort of ghosting her to baseball parks might have been the wrong move.

"Yes, I did." Luke knew it was easier to lie than to tell his mom about *another* bad date. "We had a good time."

As he sipped his water, someone hustled past their table. All he caught was the back of a green shirt and shiny brown hair. He froze, his breath still as he thought for a split second that it was Mariah.

"Honey, I said, do they still have Nathan's hot dogs at the stadium?"

Luke looked at his mother, who was staring at him expectantly.

"Uh, yeah, they do. I had a few at the game." He looked back toward the kitchen; the person who had whizzed past them earlier turned around. It wasn't Mariah.

I've got to calm down, Luke thought. *What's wrong with me?*

"Son, I don't think we told you yet... your mother and I are going to do some traveling of our own later this year," Paul said. "We're going to London!"

Luke smiled happily at his parents.

"You've been talking about that for years. Cheers!" For the second time that day, they all lifted their glasses and toasted.

"You'll have to give us some pointers," his dad said. "I know you've been to London many times on business."

Luke nodded but didn't say anything.

"Where is work taking you next?" Martha asked in between bites of fried fish. "I bet you have a big trip as soon as you get back to the city."

Luke turned and looked out the window so no one would see his face turn crimson.

As he gazed, he caught a glimpse of an older model silver Honda Civic heading away from the lodge. His dad saw it at the same time.

"Hey, that looks like the old Civic you had in high school!" Paul said. "That car is still in the wrapper." Luke chuckled at his dad's favorite saying.

"Except mine had all those stickers on the bumper." Something caught Luke's eye as the car cruised down the main road between the lodge and the lake.

In the gentle evening breeze, a relaxed arm hung out from the car's window. Fingers danced, tracing invisible patterns in the air as the sun danced across tan skin. Inside the open window, Luke could see light brown hair twirling in the wind like a tumbleweed.

He nearly dropped his fork as he watched Mariah's car fade away as she left the park.

"I think we've lost him again," Martha said, smiling at her husband.

Luke shook his head as if to clear it. "Sorry, Mom, something just caught my eye. You were saying?"

"What do you think about having a cookout with the Dyers?"

The question snapped him out of his daydream.

"The Dyers? Who's that?" He realized he'd missed an entire conversation.

"You know Sandy and Bill," his dad said. "We go to their house every year for their big Mardi Gras party."

"Of course, yes." Luke popped a French fry into his mouth. "They're coming here?"

Martha sighed.

"Sorry, Mom!" Luke laughed. "You have my full attention now."

"Sandy and Bill will be driving through the area this week on their way home from New York City. They've heard us talk about the park for years, but they've never been. So we invited them to stay a few days."

Paul winked at his son. "We'll grill out their first night and show them what park life is all about."

Martha picked up her glass of water and sipped it, studying Luke's face.

"And surely you remember their daughter Sarah..." She and her husband exchanged knowing, excited smiles.

Luke wracked his brain. He'd known quite a few Sarahs in his time, but none stood out. His thoughts returned to Mariah. He'd never known a Mariah. He shook his head no, and his mother sighed again.

"Well that answers my next question. Sarah moved to New York City six months ago. They went there to visit her, and now she's traveling back with them for a visit home."

"That sounds nice." Luke was barely able to pretend he was interested.

"I emailed you her phone number and asked you to take her out, buy her dinner, maybe show her some nice, safe places in the city."

"Oh, yeah. I never got a chance to do that." Luke hoped his mom couldn't tell that he still had no idea what she was talking about.

"That job of yours," Paul said, shaking his head. "It sounds like it doesn't allow you to have much of a social life." Once again, Luke turned and looked out the window so his father wouldn't see his face turn red.

"Maybe this week you can get to know Sarah a little. She has a lot going for her," Martha continued. She wasn't giving up. "She's studying fashion and does some modeling, her mother tells me. My gosh, you both live in the same city. How wonderful is that."

Luke's mother had always been frustrated that she never got to meet any of his girlfriends. He barely got to know them himself before he got bored or they grew impatient with him working all the time.

He glanced up from his dinner and saw the look his parents exchanged. Suddenly, he understood. If he hadn't been so lost in thought about Mariah, he would have smelled the setup a mile away.

Chapter 2

When Mariah's alarm jarred her awake at seven the next morning, she hit snooze and pulled the blanket tight over her head.

She'd barely slept last night. Closing her eyes, she had tried imagining something peaceful, like the fog hovering over Twin Pines Lake or the gentle waves lapping against the beach. She even turned on some meditative music.

But nothing erased the thoughts of Luke Anderson from her mind. That perfect smile, those piercing green eyes. Bright with excitement when he walked into the lodge yesterday afternoon. When he walked into her life.

The look in his eyes hinted at something else Mariah picked up on, but she couldn't quite pin it down. A little bit of sadness, maybe. She groaned and kicked off the covers, stretching her arms above her head as the ceiling fan moved a light breeze across her thin pink pajama shorts and camisole.

"What the heck is wrong with me?" she said aloud. "Have I gone crazy? What do I even *know* about this guy?"

Then she listened for the sounds of her elderly father moving around in the kitchen. So far, the house was quiet, except for her racing thoughts.

She grabbed a neatly folded work shirt and a pair of dark brown khaki shorts. Peeling off her pajamas, she stepped into the shower and exhaled deeply as the cool water tickled her skin and made her feel a little more alive.

A cool shower in the morning had always been her secret to waking up. She often wondered if she preferred a cold shower over a hot one because of her life spent swimming in Twin Pines Lake, whose water was always chilly even in the deepest recesses of summer.

As Mariah rinsed the shampoo from her hair and worked in conditioner, she asked herself again: "What *do* I know about Luke?"

She knew his first and last name. That was a good start. When she lived in New York City during college, she'd been on dates with guys whose last names she'd never even cared to learned.

That's another thing Mariah knew: he lived in the city. She'd seen it on the reservation. After four years in New York City for undergrad and one year for a master's program she never finished, she thought she was far enough away to never deal with *those* guys again. The ones who never left Manhattan and would rather die than spend a day at any other park than Central Park. Luke, however, clearly wasn't one of those guys.

Mariah also knew he had expensive taste. His gray V-neck shirt and black fitted jeans looked simple, but she could tell they were high-end.

And that sports car. Park guests had to include the make and model of their cars. Before she left work yesterday, she noted what the reservation said, and in her restlessness around two in the morning, she had Googled it.

As Mariah rinsed off, she smiled thinking of one more thing she knew about Luke: he had to be single, right? He wasn't wearing a ring, and who would stay in a cabin with their parents if they had a girlfriend?

~

Mariah hurriedly hung her purse in the office closet, grabbed a bottle of water from the fridge, and hopped onto the stool behind the registration desk.

Jeffrey looked at his watch dramatically and raised his eyebrows.

"I'm on time! Just barely, but I am." She held her hand in front of her mouth as she yawned. "I got distracted this morning, and then I had to get Dad situated before I left."

"How's he doing?"

Mariah shrugged. "He has his good days and his bad ones. Today seems like it's going to be a good one."

Jeffrey reached over and patted her hand.

"You're a good daughter."

Mariah felt a lump in her throat. She might have been a good daughter, but it was at the sacrifice of everything else, she sometimes felt.

They spent the next half hour fielding questions from guests: *What time does the restaurant open for lunch? Can I buy fishing bait in the gift shop?* Their morning was also peppered with the usual sounds of guests dropping their keys into the small wooden box affixed to the outside wall of the lodge, just beside the front door, labeled "Cabin key return."

Mariah felt like she could fall asleep right where she was. She hopped down off her stool and glanced at Jeffrey.

"I'm going to get some fresh air. I'll be back in five."

The lodge den's high wooden beams and fireplace gave the room a rustic, comfy feeling, as if there should always be a twelve-foot-tall Christmas tree burning bright. Families sat on the plush couches and chairs, some on their phones or reading books, others peacefully taking in the view.

The wall facing the lake was made entirely of windows and doors, and Mariah pushed open one of the doors and walked onto the patio. She sank into an empty Adirondack chair away from guests and hoped the morning breeze would awaken her senses and clear her mind.

What she had told Jeffrey was true: her father *was* having a good morning. It surprised her to even think that. In fact, for the past few weeks, he acted like he was feeling better than he'd felt all year. Maybe his new medicine was helping. They'd struggled for years to find something that would alleviate the pain and discomfort from his arthritis. She was afraid to be hopeful, but lately she couldn't help letting a little of it creep in.

Mariah reached down and flicked a sweat fly off of her leg. She smiled at the idea of having a job where she needed to wear bug repellent. She wouldn't want it any other way.

But she hadn't always been so certain. In high school, she was convinced Wall Street was where she belonged. She imagined waking up early every morning and pounding the floor of the New York Stock Exchange. She'd been obsessed with Demi Moore in the movie *Margin Call*.

Then, during her junior year of high school, her mom walked out on them. A midlife crisis, everyone said. Mariah knew that her mom had never loved their little town or the park. That was something she had never hidden, even when Mariah was a girl.

As her junior year turned into her senior year with rarely a word from her mother, Mariah would wonder every single day where she'd gone. For a few years, she received birthday cards—one from Los Angeles and another from Boise—but then they stopped.

As time went on, she didn't wonder as much where her mom had gone. Her dad was the one who needed her attention. He'd stopped taking care of himself; stopped taking his medicine and stopped being the energetic, optimistic dad she'd grown up with.

Mariah gave it four years while she went away to college for a business degree. She hoped that nearby family and friends could help him out of his rut, but halfway into the first semester of her MBA program, she knew what she had to do.

And she hadn't looked back. She wasn't one for regrets. She loved her dad, her job, and her hometown. But she would be lying to herself if she didn't admit that, deep down and despite her happiness, she was lonely.

Mariah's watch vibrated on her wrist, a reminder to head back inside. The fresh air had helped, but now as she slowly stood up from the cozy Adirondack chair, her eyes skimmed the lake, looking for any sign of Luke before she went back inside.

"How was your break? Feel better?" Jeffrey asked as she took her seat behind the desk. A little kid ran up and grabbed a park map off of the counter.

As Mariah was about to respond, Jeffrey lowered his voice.

"Are you tired because you spent the night dreaming about your mystery man?" His eyebrows wiggled up and down and he playfully grabbed Mariah's arm.

She could feel her cheeks burn hot. Deep down she was hoping Jeffrey had forgotten about Luke. She was hoping *she* would forget about him. But every time the lodge doors opened that morning, her head jerked up in anticipation that maybe, just maybe, it might be him walking in.

"How silly was that yesterday?" she said flippantly. "I probably wouldn't even recognize him if I saw him."

"Girl, please. You're telling me that if the sexiest man to ever grace Twin Pines walked into the building again, you wouldn't recognize him?"

Mariah burst out laughing.

"It's a big park!" she protested. "I see a lot of people."

Jeffrey pursed his lips and shook his head.

~

As the clock crept ever so slowly toward lunchtime, Mariah felt like she was going to jump out of her skin. Her sleep deprivation made it hard to concentrate. The rush of guest checkouts was a good distraction for a little while, but once things settled down again, her edginess returned.

She tried to do everything she could to distract herself. She rearranged the flyers and maps on the counter, meticulously straightening each stack. Then she came back behind the desk and organized the drawer that held the Twin Pines State Park souvenir pens, throwing out the dried-up ones without caps.

Content with her work, she sat still for a few moments before walking to the other side of the lobby to straighten up all the memos thumbtacked on the bulletin board. Jeffrey leaned back on his stool, arms crossed and as relaxed as ever, watching her.

"You're like a hummingbird! I can't keep up with where you are."

Mariah's plan seemed to work, except every time she felt the breeze from the front door open, her head snapped toward it with an expectant flutter in her stomach.

Then she immediately felt embarrassed at the disappointment she felt when Luke did not walk through the door. Luke, she reminded herself, that she'd only met once for maybe five minutes. Her entire body was flooded with more embarrassment. She was almost twenty-nine, which in her book meant she was too old for these types of emotions.

Just as Mariah decided to rearrange the chairs around the tables in the den, Simone Carter, the park superintendent, approached the front desk.

"I hate to ask, but everyone on the maintenance crew is out on calls." She held up a single light bulb. "Could one of you take this to a guest? Their refrigerator light has gone out, and I'd like to get it to them as quickly as possible."

As Jeffrey opened his mouth to answer, Mariah leaped up. She was in such a rush that her foot got tangled in the leg of the stool.

"I'll take it!" She hobbled behind the desk, trying to disentangle her foot. Jeffrey and Simone watched her with wide eyes.

Finally, she opened a drawer and grabbed the keys to one of the park pickup trucks. She scurried around to the front of the desk and grabbed the light bulb out of Simone's hand as she rushed toward the front door.

"Wait!" Simone said as Mariah ran by. "You don't even know which cabin!"

And as she slowed down, just a little, Mariah heard her say: cabin fifteen on East Meadows Trail.

~

Last night, long after his parents went inside, Luke sat around the campfire, moving the embers around and keeping it alive into the early morning. He was mesmerized by the warmth and light, and he couldn't remember the last time he'd been around a campfire. Probably more than five years ago, he imagined, which was the last time he was at Twin Pines.

The flames danced and flickered, casting a soft, warm glow that illuminated the surrounding night. The crackling sound of burning wood and the occasional pop of the embers almost put him in a trance.

And every now and then, he would hear a rustling and look into the woods, shining his flashlight. Two bright eyes shone back at him, a masked face emerging from the foliage. Luke laughed and shoved his granola bar deeper in his pocket.

Despite going to bed late, he had woken early, even before his parents. He quietly slipped into his exercise clothes and grabbed his running shoes, lacing them up on the cabin porch.

The slow jog around the lake felt good. Luke moved with a relaxed and steady pace, his breath forming misty puffs in the cool air as he followed the winding path. The rising sun cast a gentle golden hue on the water, and for Luke, it seemed like he was the only person in the world awake.

Still, at the sound of any car nearby, he turned to see if it could be Mariah. He figured it was too early for her shift, but he had to be sure.

When he returned from his jog, he was surprised to see his parents up.

"We want to hike Bearpaw Trail before it gets too hot," Paul said. "Want to come with us?"

"I'll pass this time. I'm worn out from my run. Maybe we can meet up and go bird watching after lunch."

"That should work for us," his mom said. "You look tired. You were outside pretty late, weren't you?"

Luke nodded. "It was nice just sitting underneath the stars. I didn't want to let the fire die."

As his parents walked out the door, Martha had one request.

"If you go to the lodge today, can you check the gift shop and see if they sell can openers? We forgot to pack one."

Once his parents were gone, Luke looked around the cabin and tried to figure out his next move. When he was a kid, he couldn't wait to jump down from his bunk each morning and spend the day on his bicycle. He wouldn't come back until the next mealtime.

But this morning, staying inside felt like a good idea. Maybe it was the run, or maybe it was his lack of sleep, but he felt more tired than his thirty-two-year-old body should. He kept waiting for that little boy's enthusiasm and drive to fire up inside him. He hoped, deep down, it was still there.

"Let's do something I haven't tried in a very long time," Luke said out loud. He rummaged through his duffel bag until he found what he was looking for. "Let's read a book."

It was already beginning to feel warm. Between the time the sun rose until it was hidden behind tall evergreens, the cabin's thin white curtains did very little to block the heat.

Luke turned on a well-worn box fan and aimed it at his bunk. He climbed up into his bed, arranged his pillows, and settled in with *The Great Gatsby*.

Just a few pages in, he still felt warm. He jumped down from the bunk and aimed the fan even more toward his bed until he saw the corners of the sheet rustling softly in the breeze.

"That's better." He climbed back up the ladder.

Moments later, Luke blinked furiously as a bead of sweat trickled into his eyelash.

"Dang it! That does it."

Checking the time, he knew his parents would be hiking for a few more hours. So he did the only thing left he could think to do: he took off all his clothes, leaving only his navy-blue boxer briefs. Lying back against the pillow, he barely made it to the description of the town of West Egg before he was sound asleep.

But moments later, he awoke to the sound of a car coming up the gravel driveway. Before he could move, it was quiet.

"Must have been one of the cars at the cabin next door," he mumbled and sat up straighter, reaching for his book.

He heard another sound and paused. It sounded like a squeak. He listened intently, his eyes searching the floor and kitchen countertops for a mouse or chipmunk that had made its way inside.

Suddenly, before Luke had time to think, the door of the cabin flew open. And there was Mariah, wide-eyed and holding a light bulb in her hand.

Luke sat in his underwear on the edge of his bunk bed, unable to speak.

"Here, take this," she stammered, looking around the room.

With her cheeks burning red, Mariah finally placed the light bulb on top of the refrigerator and ran out of the cabin almost as quickly as she had entered, leaving the door wide open behind her.

~

"Oh my god oh my god oh my god," Mariah muttered as she hastily made her way down the porch stairs and toward the pickup truck. She had left the driver's door open and the engine running, as if a quick escape had been imminent.

"Wait! Mariah!" Luke's voice emanated from inside the cabin. Then he was on the porch, this time with shorts on and a T-shirt in hand. In one smooth motion, he placed his arms through the shirt's sleeves and lowered it down over his body. Before the blue fabric settled in place, Mariah caught a glimpse of his toned midsection.

Her right leg was in the truck and she was just hoisting herself into the driver's seat. "I'm so sorry. I didn't think anyone was home. I saw the car but there were no lights on and it was so quiet. I should have..."

"It's okay." Luke squinted against the sun as he walked toward the truck. He held up the light bulb. "Thanks for this. My mom will be happy."

"You're welcome. Sorry it, uhm, took so long."

"I would say it was worth the wait."

Mariah felt flustered. Beads of sweat formed on her upper lip. She looked at Luke, studying his face, unsure what to do next. She must have had a confused look on her face.

"We've... we've met before," Luke said, staring intently at her. "I'm Luke." He reached out his hand.

Mariah burst out laughing.

"Oh, I remember you, Luke. Trust me, I remember you."

Her stomach flipped at the cocky grin that appeared on Luke's face.

"Look, why don't you turn that ignition off and stay for a while... I mean, for a few."

Mariah couldn't stop the huge smile from spreading across her face. She closed the truck door and followed Luke toward the front porch.

"Do you always bust in unannounced into cabins like that? If I hadn't been here, would you have stolen my wallet?" He turned around and flashed that same cocky grin.

Mariah's face flushed an even deeper pink.

"Actually, I don't." She tried to come up with something witty. "Honestly, I don't know why I didn't knock. I've got nothing. I didn't sleep well last night, and my brain isn't working."

Luke's eyebrows lifted slightly with intrigue.

"Why didn't you sleep well?"

Mariah was caught off guard by the question. Especially because the reason she hadn't slept was him. And now, he was standing before her, just as handsome as she remembered: bent slightly at the waist, resting his elbows on the porch railing and juggling the light bulb back and forth between his hands lightly like a baseball.

"I have a lot on my mind."

Mariah could feel the tension, even in the middle of the wilderness where the air moved freely. Birds chirped loudly around them, a woodpecker making its presence known from a perch high in a nearby tree.

She decided to try and change the subject.

"How's your trip so far? This is a nice cabin. I like how it sits back off the trail."

"This is the cabin my family always stays in. Ever since I was a baby."

"You mentioned that. I remember you saying that when you checked in."

"I did?" Luke's eyebrows knitted in concentration.

Mariah felt a vibration in her pocket. She reached into it and looked at her phone. Her calendar reminder said, "Lunch break."

"I have to run," she said, turning on her heel. "My break just started." Normally she packed food, but she'd felt so sluggish and rushed that morning that she hadn't had time.

"Are you going back to the lodge?" Luke asked.

Mariah turned around and looked at him, lifting her sunglasses off her face and resting them on her head.

"Yeah, I'll probably grab something from the restaurant. Would you... would you like to join me?"

The words came out before she could stop them, and she stood still in disbelief at what she'd just done.

"Sure, but only under one condition," Luke replied.

Her heart skipped a beat.

"What's that?"

Instead of answering, he disappeared inside. Seconds later he emerged, this time wearing shoes. He had his cabin key, and she could see the square imprint of his wallet in his shorts pocket.

"That I get to ride in this fancy pickup truck of yours."

Before Mariah had a chance to respond, Luke hurried to the passenger's side.

"Well, okay then!" she said, her head spinning as his door slammed.

Chapter 3

Mariah steered the pickup truck into a parking spot marked "Park Vehicles Only." Even though the ride from Luke's cabin was three minutes at most, she hadn't been able to think of anything smart or clever or cute to say. Instead, she let her arm hang out the window and enjoyed the breeze blowing through her fingers.

Luke didn't seem to mind at all. She had the courage to peek at him once, and she caught him looking out his window with a smile on his face. It made her stomach feel like it was full of bubbles.

"Here, let me get that for you." Luke reached to open the lodge front door. "It's still as heavy as it was when I was a kid." He grunted dramatically as he opened it, and Mariah laughed.

"I remember that, too. I would pull and pull and finally get it. I didn't realize until years later that my dad was helping me."

"You went to the park as a kid?"

She nodded. "I grew up in Owenton, the next town over."

Once inside, the first person Mariah saw was Jeffrey, who was reading a paperback copy of *The Seven Husbands of Evelyn Hugo*.

"Mariah!" he said happily, laying the book face down. Then his mouth dropped open and his eyes grew wide.

"Hi," she said with a sheepish smile as Luke appeared from behind her. Jeffrey didn't say anything, but his eyes moved quickly between the two. "Luke, this is my friend Jeffrey. We've worked here together for years."

Jeffrey finally blinked and closed his mouth a little. He gingerly grabbed Luke's hand and squeezed it, but he still hadn't uttered a word.

Mariah looked at the clock on the wall. She didn't want to be rushed during lunch, but if she waited any longer, that's exactly what would happen. And who knows if she'd get another chance to make a good impression, especially after the light bulb disaster.

"We're going to grab a bite upstairs, and then I'll be back down. I might be five minutes late, but no more than that."

She walked slowly away, looking over her shoulder at Jeffrey to make sure he heard her. She thought he had, but she couldn't be sure because he still hadn't spoken. Finally, she rounded the corner, and Jeffrey and the front desk disappeared, as she ascended the stairs to the restaurant.

She headed toward a table with a view of the lake. Under the noon sun, it glistened like a sheet of liquid diamonds, its surface rippling gently in the breeze. People dotted the shoreline, some fishing, others lounging on the grassy banks with blankets spread around them.

"It never gets old, does it," Luke said, and Mariah didn't even have to look at him to know that he was talking about the view.

"Never."

"I've never seen anything so beautiful," he added. This time, instead of looking out the window, he was looking at her. She cleared her throat and studied the menu, sliding another one across the table.

A few minutes later, Luke handed his menu to Sally, their waitress. "I'll take the loaded French fries."

"And I'll have the grilled cheese sandwich, just the sandwich,"

Mariah said. She knew how big the loaded fries were, and she eagerly anticipated helping Luke eat his. As long as that wasn't too forward.

Sally, who had worked at the restaurant for a long time, looked dreamily at Luke, then winked at Mariah.

"Ok, thanks, Sally!" she said in an effort to make her leave and then turned her attention toward Luke.

Mariah was nervous. This felt like a first date, and she'd never been on a first date without having known it was happening ahead of time. Normally, she was able to shower, blow out her hair, put on makeup, and pick out something cute to wear. Today, she hadn't even had time to look in the mirror. For all she knew, she had breakfast on her shirt and her hair was a hot mess.

What a day it had been. It was all she could do to not roll her eyes. First she walked in on Luke practically naked. Strike one. Then the first time they really got to talk and get to know each other, she was in her wrinkled work outfit and driving around in the park pickup. Strike two.

Whatever happens, it'll be okay, she said to herself. *If he excuses himself to go to the restroom and never comes back, you'll know why.*

She nervously played with the straw wrapper, wadding it up in a little ball and then straightening it out again.

"How's your trip going? If you're like everyone else who comes here in the summer, you've been looking forward to it since, oh, probably January."

"Yeah, I guess so..." Luke said hesitantly.

"I know this one woman who has been coming here for twenty years. She has a handwritten packing list that she re-uses. She adds one or two things to it after each trip. You can barely read it."

"Are you talking about my mom?" Luke laughed. "Actually, I haven't been looking forward to this trip."

Mariah looked at him questioningly.

"That's not exactly what I meant," he said, shaking his head. "Let me try that again. I didn't decide to come here until a few days ago. It was a spur of the moment decision."

Mariah could feel there was more to this story.

"I remember you said you hadn't been here in five years," she said. "That's a long time for someone who once came every year!"

"It's been hard to get away the past few years. I traveled a lot for my job. And when I wasn't traveling, I was in the office working nonstop. At one point, I had about seventy-five people reporting to me."

"That sounds stressful," Mariah said. "And fun..." Her plans to work on Wall Street briefly crossed her mind. At one point in her life, Luke's job had been *her* dream.

"And then there's this thing about New York City," Luke added. "Everything you want or need is right there. There's no reason to leave."

"You probably wouldn't understand." He looked around the restaurant and out the window. "Living here, it's so different."

"What makes you think I wouldn't understand?" She sat up straighter in her chair.

"I'm sorry." He looked nervous. "I just, I assumed..."

"We just met, you shouldn't assume anything about me."

Mariah paused for a few seconds and then she laughed.

"I'm just giving you a hard time. Sort of," she smiled. "I went to college in New York City. I lived there for almost five years. I know what the city is like. Trust me."

Luke's eyes widened. "Wow. So what brought you back here?"

"Family stuff." She didn't really want to talk about it. She never did. Sally set down plates in front of them, then briskly disappeared to another table.

"These loaded fries are insane," Luke said. "I'll never eat all of these. You'll have to help me."

"I'll do what I can to help."

"What kind of family stuff, if you don't mind me asking," he said as he popped a French fry into his mouth.

"It's not a big deal." She looked at her watch. She had ten minutes to learn all she could about Luke before she went back to work and possibly never saw him again. She felt like Cinderella, and her carriage was about to turn into a pumpkin.

"Your job sounds nice," she said, changing the subject. "I went to business school for a year after undergrad."

"Wow, business school is a big departure from working here," Luke said. "No offense, but I think your skills are being underutilized behind that registration desk."

Mariah laughed.

"At the end of each month, I work with the director of the park on financial statements and preparing reports for the Board. I still get to do some of the things I miss."

Luke nodded. "Even so, I can't imagine a better greeting than seeing your smiling face."

Mariah felt her neck and face turn crimson, and a tingle of excitement coursed through her body. It was the first time since they'd sat down that she felt like their impromptu date-ish thing was going well.

"What your career looks like is what I would have killed for back then. To me, that was the dream life," Mariah said. "All that international travel."

A look of sadness filled Luke's green eyes.

"What? I'm happy now, I just told you. Don't give me that pity look."

"No, that's not..." Luke started. "Sorry, no, no pity look here."

"Okay, good. As I was saying, all that travel... where are you headed next?"

Luke's shoulders sank lower and his eyebrows came together in a scowl. Before she could stop herself, before she remembered that she didn't really know him and that they'd just met, Mariah reached across the table and put her hand on top of his. She squeezed it gently.

"What's wrong?"

Luke looked up from his plate and into Mariah's eyes, his eyebrows knitted tightly.

"It's just... I haven't told anyone about this, not even my parents, but before this trip, I actually lost my job. Like, three days ago."

~

Luke couldn't believe what just came out of his mouth. Their lunch had been going *so* well. And now he just revealed to Mariah that he was the biggest loser in the world.

"Oh no, I'm so sorry to hear that." A look of concern filled her pretty face. "What happened?"

He wished he could take it back and not have to explain anything. But he'd started this, so he needed to power through.

"It's a bit of a mess, honestly. We merged with another company and there was a lot of overlap, and my position was one of the ones that got eliminated."

"That's really tough."

"I didn't see it coming at all. I've been with that company for years, and now it feels like everything's just been turned upside down."

"That's the *worst* feeling," Mariah said.

Luke shook his head. "I put so much effort into my work, and now it's all gone." He looked around the room and out the window, suddenly angry. "I sacrificed *so much* for that place. I gave up things I didn't want to give up."

He took a long drink of his water. He was starting to feel different than he had a few moments ago. His shoulders were relaxing and his breathing was even again. Surprisingly, he began to feel a sense of relief.

Is it possible that spilling my guts to Mariah was the right move? Luke thought to himself.

"You're the first person I've talked to about this. My mom and dad are so happy I came on this trip that they hadn't even asked me how I got the time to come after years of not being able to."

"Well, I hope you at least got a big severance."

"It wasn't bad, actually. Thanks for pointing out an upside. Sometimes it's hard to find them when you're in the middle of it."

"Here's another upside," Mariah said, gesturing around the restaurant and then looking at the lake. "If you can't find another job in the city, you can always work here. We could put your over-qualifications to work alongside mine!"

Luke suddenly felt like he'd had the wind knocked out of him. He couldn't speak.

"I'm just kidding!" Mariah said. "Geez, sorry. You're trying to be serious and I'm over here making jokes."

Before he could gather himself, Mariah looked at her watch and her demeanor changed. She pulled some cash from her pocket and laid it on the table.

"I have to get back to work or Jeffrey's going to storm up here." She stood up and started to walk away, then came back and paused, as if she was unsure what to do or say next.

Luke suddenly felt her warm hand on his shoulder.

"Take care. Maybe I'll see you around." And then she disappeared down the stairs.

Luke's head was spinning. Mariah had left in such a hurry that he looked at where she'd been sitting, half expecting to see a glass slipper lying there.

~

When Mariah walked out of the lodge later that evening, she breathed a sigh of relief. She felt exhausted.

Usually she would rush home after work, but she'd called her father and found out he had visitors and that they'd brought dinner. It made her happy. For the longest time, he hadn't had the energy for company.

Mariah was even happier that this freed up her evening. She decided to drive to the beach and try to relax. Popping her trunk in the parking lot, Mariah grabbed a king-sized blanket she always kept there. Then she slipped on flip flops and walked toward the concession stand.

"One scoop of Rocky Road in a cup, with a cone on the side, please."

A moment later, the young woman wearing the same polo Mariah was wearing brought out the ice cream. She'd had the same job during her summers in high school. That's where she'd learned the ice cream trick. Cups could hold a bigger scoop of ice cream than a cone could. Once you ordered the cone on the side, you could then carefully flip the cup upside down on the cone.

Mariah found an empty spot close to the water to spread her blanket. She closed her eyes and tilted her face toward the warm June sun. The day had been an emotional rollercoaster. Her lunch with Luke had been totally random and sort of fun, until he dropped the bomb about his job.

She hadn't expected for the lunch to turn so serious. Afterwards, when she went back downstairs, Jeffrey had peppered her with a million questions. Instead of feeling excited to talk about her date thing, she just kind of wanted to forget it happened.

But now, what she also didn't expect was to care so much about what Luke had told her.

In what world should she be concerned with some rich New York

City businessman who lost his high-power job? He'd find another one quicker than anyone else she knew, plus, he was getting a severance package! And probably a nice one, too.

What does he have to complain about? Mariah thought. *He's in better shape than most.*

Just when Mariah had decided she wouldn't waste her time feeling bad for him, she remembered his crestfallen face: that furrowed brow, those eyes that were sparkling and happy just the day before. At lunch, his shoulders hunched forward, as if the weight of his burden was pulling his whole body forward.

She'd felt bad running off so quickly, but she didn't want to get in trouble. If *she* got fired, she wouldn't get a severance payout.

Mariah wiggled her toes into the soft sand. As the sun kissed her skin, she took a bite of ice cream. The chill of it sent a shiver of delight through her.

There was one other thing about their conversation that was nagging at Mariah. When she jokingly suggested that Luke get a job at Twin Pines, his face had changed instantly.

She hadn't meant to offend him. In the moment, she had felt like they shared something in common: that feeling of suddenly being lost when you thought you were on the right path. She had meant for her comment to break the tension, not to be flippant and uncaring.

As she ate her ice cream and watched the happy people around her, she could feel the certainty deep inside: She'd probably not see Luke again until he was checking out of his cabin at the end of the week and heading back to his regular life in New York City.

Mariah shuddered at the idea of appearing uncaring. Because for the life of her—and she couldn't figure out how and why—she *did* care for Luke Anderson, this man she'd only met yesterday. More than she should.

She sighed. Tomorrow was a new day to try to make sense of it all.

And for today, all that mattered was appreciating the beauty of the evening and enjoying the rest of that ice cream cone.

Chapter 4

Luke didn't expect to feel like this when he woke up the next morning. It was six o'clock, and he opened his eyes hesitantly and listened for the sounds of his parents shuffling around.

He felt *terrific*, like a weight had been lifted.

At first he'd tossed and turned, going through his conversation with Mariah over and over in his head. He'd said too much. If that had actually been a first date, it would have been a dramatic failure. She would have run screaming from the restaurant, leaving him with her bill to pay and never returning.

But after a solid night's rest, Luke woke up with a different perspective. He hadn't realized that he'd simply needed to tell someone about losing his job. And not just anyone. Even though they were getting to know each other a little more each day, he knew enough to realize that she was special. And it wasn't just her beauty. It was what he saw in her eyes every time he looked into them. And the hint of mystery around her.

This morning, the only regret he felt was that he hadn't learned enough about her. He'd done all the talking and hadn't asked her many questions.

As he poured a cup of coffee, he decided he had to see her again. Lost in thought, he was jerked back to reality with the slam of the screen door.

"You're up!" his dad said. "The kayaks are in the car. We're ready when you are."

"Oh!" Luke said. He'd completely forgotten that they had decided on an early-morning kayaking trip around the lake. "I'll be ready in fifteen." He'd been so spacey all week, and he didn't want his parents to think he'd forgotten yet another thing they'd planned to do together. He'd already forgotten to buy a can opener from the gift shop the other day, like he'd promised his mom.

A half hour later, as the sun began to paint the sky pink and gold, Luke and his parents eagerly carried their kayaks from their cars to the edge of Twin Pines Lake. The air was crisp and filled with the promise of a tranquil morning on the water.

The three of them carefully secured their life vests and paddles. Luke's heart raced with excitement. The water had always been a special place for his family, a serene oasis nestled between the rolling hills.

And for the first time since arriving, Luke felt truly happy. More at peace than he'd felt in a while.

The early morning mist clung to the lake's surface, creating an ethereal ambiance that enveloped them. Martha and Paul paddled in graceful tandem, their strokes synchronized as if they were an extension of each other. In his own kayak, Luke sipped hot coffee from the travel mug he'd brought with him and enjoyed the serenity.

As they glided along, the only sounds were the dips of their paddles and the occasional call of a distant bird. The water's surface reflected the changing colors of the morning sky, transforming the lake into a breathtaking canvas.

Luke felt a sense of awe and gratitude as he paddled beside his parents. Their shared love for nature and adventure had always brought them closer, and moments like these were a testament to their bond. A bond he'd lost track of over the years.

As the sun's first rays stretched across the horizon, Paul pointed to a cluster of trees near the shoreline.

"Let's park over there and have some breakfast." Luke's stomach growled as he eagerly headed in that direction. Once on shore, Martha opened the lid of a small cooler and handed everyone a sandwich.

"Simple PB&Js. When you were a kid, Luke, you would eat these for every meal while we were here."

"I might start doing that again. I forgot how good they are!"

"We'll be eating even better for dinner," Paul said. "The Dyers get here this evening, and we'll have a big cookout. Hamburgers, hot dogs, I might even buy some steaks while we're in town."

Luke's heart sank. He'd forgotten today was when Sarah and her parents were coming. He sighed, thinking about how his time was already spoken for. How would he sneak away so he could try to see Mariah?

~

By the time early afternoon rolled around, Luke was worn out. After kayaking, he'd gone into town with his mother to help her with preparation for the big cookout.

First they'd purchased extra firewood for roasting marshmallows after dinner. Then they went to Palmer's Market, where Martha painstakingly chose the perfect ears of corn, pounds of hamburger, and bags of potato chips.

They also ran into the general store and bought decorations: a festive tablecloth, napkins, plastic dinnerware, balloons, and citronella candles. It was important to Martha that the Dyers had a good time.

Back at the cabin, Luke's thoughts raced. He didn't understand what the big deal was with tonight's cookout. Unless Sarah was the one his parents were really trying to impress. He rolled his eyes at the thought. He was unconcerned; he still hadn't had a chance to find Mariah. To see her again, to talk to her, to make sure that he hadn't scared her away.

Then he had a realization. *So what if I scared her? So what if she doesn't want to see me again. What does it even matter? I'll be leaving in a few days. What's the point of any of this anyway?*

Luke was suddenly feeling confused, the thoughts that had been racing around his head all day colliding. He'd come to Twin Pines to get away from his troubles at home and had fallen into another kind of problem.

A problem named Mariah, who had the most beautiful smile he'd ever seen. Just the thought of how her hand had felt yesterday on top of his gave him goosebumps.

"I'll be right back," he said, startling his mom.

"Wait, where are you going? I still need you and your father's help with everything."

"Don't worry, I'll be back before you know it." Luke grabbed his beach bag.

A twenty-minute walk later, he stood at the beach's edge, the memories of his childhood summers flooding back as he gazed out at the pier. The sun's rays danced on the water, and a gentle breeze ruffled his hair, carrying with it the faint scent of pine.

Taking a deep breath, he felt a rush of excitement course through his body. He had done this countless times before, but today, there was a sense of nostalgia that gripped him. The lake, the pier, the cool water: they all held a special place in his heart, a repository of his most cherished memories.

With each step into the lake, the cold water crept higher up his legs.

He let out a chuckle, his heart lightening as he remembered the countless times he and his friends had dared each other to swim to the pier.

Those were the days. When you made friends for a week, then you went back home with only happy memories until you returned the next summer to do it all over again. Sometimes you saw the same friends, but more often than not, you just made new ones.

When Luke reached the pier, he pulled himself onto it and stood there for a moment, the rough wood familiar beneath his feet. He could feel the ghosts of his childhood, his friends splashing and laughing, their voices echoing in the recesses of his mind.

He took a few steps back, his heart pounding with excitement. Closing his eyes for a brief moment, the sounds of the lake and the warmth of the sun washed over him. Then, without hesitation, he sprinted forward, his body instinctively knowing the way.

The air rushed past him as he soared over the water, a split second of weightlessness before he plunged into the freezing lake. Luke kicked and paddled, breaking the surface with a gasp, his laughter mingling with the lapping of the waves. He opened his eyes wide and wiped the water off his face.

As he swam back toward the shore, the sense of nostalgia lingered. His swim turned into a walk as he reached the beach, and with a contented sigh, Luke shook his head, sending droplets of water sparkling into the air.

"Now," he said out loud. "It's time for ice cream."

~

"Was that...?" Jeffrey said. He stood behind the counter of the beach concession stand, halfway through restacking cups and straws. He paused and stared.

"It sure was," Mariah said, a knowing smile spreading across her face.

They watched as Luke emerged from the water. Even from the concession stand, they could see he was shivering.

"He's gritting his teeth," Jeffrey said. "He must be freezing."

But Mariah knew better. She could tell that Luke was smiling. Or at least trying to. Anyone who had spent their childhoods at Twin Pines knew the magical pull of the pier. It was a rite of passage for every kid to swim out there and jump into the ice cold water. Mariah remembered the first time she mustered the courage to do it when she was fourteen.

Her father had taught her how to swim, so she had no qualms about getting to the pier. As she stood there, though, her heart raced. With her friends cheering her on from the beach, she took a deep breath, held her nose, and leaped into the air. The initial shock of the cold water took her breath away, but the thrill of the jump was invigorating.

As she resurfaced, she felt a sense of pride: now she truly was a Twin Pines native. After that, jumping off the pier became as easy as hopping on a bicycle and riding away.

Mariah watched as Luke walked back to a towel and bag he had thrown on the grass. He shook his head from side to side, flecks of water glistening in the sun.

She and Jeffrey were mesmerized. Luke's body glistened under the sunlight, highlighting his lean muscles. His physique was strong and defined, his skin lightly flushed from the exercise and the cold water.

"You know, you've been on one date with that man, and this is the second time you've seen him in pretty much just a pair of undies," Jeffrey said. "I wish my love life was this exciting."

Mariah lost it. She doubled over with laughter, and tears streamed down her face. Every time she looked at Jeffrey, she began laughing again.

"The whole beach can hear you," he whispered. "The teenagers are pointing. I'm already embarrassed enough having to work with them at this concession stand."

Because it was such a beautiful day, the beach was packed with more families than usual, and the concessions manager had asked Jeffrey to help out. He begrudgingly said yes, and Mariah decided to spend her lunch with her friend for moral support.

She had just started eating a hot dog and potato chips when they saw Luke, and now she turned her attention back to her lunch.

"I thought that laugh sounded familiar," a voice said.

Mariah whipped her head around and was met with Luke's sparkling green eyes and bright smile. He was now wearing a T-shirt, and his beach bag was hoisted onto his shoulder.

"Hey," she said, as excitement flurried through her body.

"Hey yourself," Luke said. "And Jeffrey, hello."

Jeffrey waved from behind the counter.

"So," Luke said, looking around. "What are you doing over here?"

"Lunch break. Jeffrey had to do concession duty, so I thought I'd come and support him." She smiled at her friend, who looked like he wanted to crawl under a rock.

"After I finished up here, I was going to swing by the lodge and see if you were working," Luke said. "Good thing I heard your hyena laugh across the beach, otherwise, I'd have made that trip for nothing."

Mariah almost choked on a potato chip. She looked at Jeffrey and then back at Luke.

"Hyena laugh?!"

Jeffrey was covering his mouth so she couldn't see how hard he was laughing. Before Mariah could say anything else, she was struck speechless by just how handsome Luke's was. His forehead was covered in a cascade of tousled, wet hair. His eyebrows, slightly furrowed as he struggled to suppress a smile, drew attention to his expressive green eyes.

Those eyes. Mariah thought they were his best feature, and she was certain there was a deeper layer to him beneath the composed exterior. Well, mostly composed. She'd caught a glimpse of that vulnerability yesterday.

Snap out of it, Mariah said to herself. She gathered her lunch and shoved what was left into a paper bag.

"I'm going to walk back to the lodge," she said to Jeffrey. "I'll see you later." She then smiled at Luke, and without a word, he fell in step beside her.

"Why is it that we always manage to run into each other when you're on break?" he asked. "Maybe we should meet some other time so you're not always having to rush away."

Mariah's heart skipped a beat.

"I'd love that."

As they rounded the curve of the sidewalk, a young girl on a scooter zipped toward them. Luke reached out and placed his hand on the small of Mariah's back, quickly moving her out of the way.

"That was close!" she said, feeling a little flustered. Five minutes ago, she knew how to walk, and now Luke probably thought she was helpless. Still... she didn't shrug away from his touch. His hand, which was still placed on her low black, felt warm.

"So, Mariah..." Luke said, and he dropped his hand to his side. "Tell me more about your life in New York City."

She smiled softly. Despite everything, she had loved her time in the city. It hit her as she walked along the lake path: no one ever asked her about it anymore. When she first moved back home and started her career at the park, everyone she met wanted to hear the glamorous details about the big city.

That had dried up pretty quickly. But now, Luke seemed genuinely interested. Tying back her hair with a rubber band she always kept around her wrist, she slowed her pace and looked at him with a nostalgic smile.

"I think I told you, I moved there for college and fell in love with it. Every corner seemed to have its own story to tell."

She paused, lost in her memories.

"The skyscrapers, the bustling streets, the constant hum of activity, it was like a whole different world. I used to spend my weekends exploring different neighborhoods. And the food!"

Luke smiled. "A lot more options than that hot dog you have there."

Mariah looked down at the bag and laughed. She'd forgotten she was carrying it.

"Did you have any favorite spots? Maybe I've been to a few of them."

Her face lit up. "There was this cozy little café in Greenwich Village that served the most amazing breakfast, I can't remember its name now. And a hole-in-the-wall pizzeria in Brooklyn Heights that was the best I've ever had."

"Wait."

Mariah stopped walking when she realized that Luke had stopped, too.

"Are you talking about Luigi's Pizza on Henry Street?"

"Yes!" Mariah nearly screamed. "How do you know about Luigi's?"

"I used to live just around the corner, on Clark!"

Mariah shook her head. "My friends and I used to go there early in the morning, after having way too much fun all night. We'd go out in Lower Manhattan, then take the subway to Brooklyn Heights. Just for the pizza."

"You know it's good food when you'll change boroughs for it," Luke laughed.

He suddenly got a faraway look in his eyes. Mariah's stomach sank a little. Was all this talk about New York City backfiring? Was he going to jump in his car today and drive back to his life there and never look back?

Nevertheless, it felt good to reminisce, especially as she walked the path back to the lodge, her current job and her immediate surroundings a stark contrast to her past life.

"There was this sense of empowerment that came with living there," she added as the lodge came into view through the pines. "The city taught me to appreciate the beauty in chaos."

She became quiet as she looked around at the lush green pine trees and the fluffy white clouds mirrored in the glittering lake. "It taught me to appreciate the beauty here, too."

Mariah could tell by the look on Luke's face that he understood. She took a deep breath and sighed peacefully as they walked up the hill.

"Well, this is me," she laughed when they reached the lodge porch. "I have to run off again, just like last time."

"That's a shame. I could listen to your stories all day."

Mariah blushed. "What are your plans for later? It's going to be a beautiful evening."

"My family's having a cookout. Over at the picnic tables by Beehunter Trail."

"That sounds fun!"

"I don't know about that," Luke said. "Friends of the family are visiting the park. I think it's all a ruse so my parents can set me up with their friends' daughter, Sarah."

As soon as the words came out of Luke's mouth, he looked like he wished he could take them back. He stared at his feet and kicked a rock into the grass.

Mariah felt her stomach drop a little. "Oh... really?"

Luke looked up at her.

"It's silly, it's nothing. She lives in the city, my parents have been trying to set me up with her for months. I never had the time to go out with her because I was working so..."

He let his sentence trail off. But Mariah finished it in her head: *Because I was working so much.*

And now, she thought, *while he explored new career opportunities, he'd have time to date her.*

"Don't you have to get back inside?" Luke said, his voice snapping Mariah out of her daze.

"Yeah." She looked at him, shielding her eyes from the sun. "Well, have fun tonight."

As she briskly turned toward the lodge, she felt him lightly grab her elbow.

"All I want is for it to be tomorrow and for us to go on a real date," he said with a smile. Then he leaned forward and gently kissed her on the cheek.

Mariah stood there, confused and stunned, as Luke hoisted his beach bag higher on his shoulder and walked away.

Chapter 5

Luke walked up the gravel road of East Meadows Trail. His steps were light and bouncy, and the hands of the summer breeze swiftly pushed him up the incline and around the corner toward his cabin.

Or at least that's how he felt. He didn't even mind the sweat rolling down his forehead or his loudly growling stomach.

Mariah had looked just as beautiful as she did yesterday, in her simple Twin Pines shirt and khaki shorts. He smiled and shook his head. He'd never seen her in real clothes, but he couldn't imagine her being any more beautiful.

At first he'd cursed himself for bringing up the cookout—and for bringing up Sarah—but he'd worked up the courage to tell her that he wanted to see her again. And for real this time; not random run-ins around the park.

When Luke approached his cabin, he was startled to see another car in the driveway, and then he remembered: The Dyers were here! His mother had expected him back sooner to help finish setting up.

Sheepishly, he climbed the porch steps and opened the screen door. He could hear laughter and conversation before he even stepped inside.

"Luke!" his ever-cheerful dad rang out, clapping him on the back. "Glad you could make it, son." He laughed, and Luke could tell he'd already enjoyed a beer. Looking around, he decided he could use one himself.

Sunlight filtered through the tall trees outside, casting warm golden hues across the room. The fans were on high, battling the height of the afternoon heat.

Seated at the picnic table was Mr. Dyer, a portly man with a friendly demeanor, engrossed in a conversation with Martha. Nearby, Mrs. Dyer was making herself comfortable in one of the wooden armchairs, a content smile on her face as she admired the simple beauty of the cabin.

Luke's gaze then fell upon Sarah, who was perched delicately on the edge of another wooden armchair, her posture impeccable and her expression a mingling of curiosity and slight disdain. With her jet-black hair cascading in perfectly styled waves and her makeup flawlessly applied, it was evident that Sarah ran with the fashionable crowd in New York City.

Even today, her outfit was a testament to her high-end taste: a designer sundress that seemed far too delicate for the rugged outdoors and metallic gold sandals that gleamed as if they'd never touched anything less pristine than the marble floor of her towering apartment lobby.

Luke couldn't help but feel a twinge of curiosity and bemusement. He had spent countless summers in this cabin, and the dissonance between her appearance and her surroundings was striking. What else was striking was the difference between Sarah and Mariah. Before he'd met Mariah, Sarah was exactly the kind of woman he'd be interested in.

Now, even as sophisticated and beautiful as Sarah appeared to be, it was Mariah who was front and center in his mind.

Luke stood just inside the door as Sarah rose and slowly approached him.

"You're the mysterious Luke." A small smile tugged at the corners of her mouth. "Charmed."

Luke grabbed the hand she offered and shook it gently.

Their eyes met for a brief moment, his curious and hers appraising, before she looked away with a dismissive smile.

"Nice to meet you, as well," Luke replied, feeling slightly nervous.

~

Later that afternoon, the Andersons and the Dyers parked their cars in the gravel lot next to the picnic shelters at Beehunter Trail.

The shelters were green, the same color as the cabins, and they had been scratched and etched into over the years with initials, declarations of love, phone numbers, and some unfortunate sentiments better left unsaid.

Luke helped his parents unload their car. As he hoisted a big bag of charcoal into his arms, he looked around. He was always looking for Mariah. He did it subconsciously; his mind just knew he wanted to catch a glimpse of her. He peered toward the beach, wondering if she had returned to the concession stand to see Jeffrey. But it was too far away for him to tell.

As he sat the bag of charcoal on the ground next to an old grill, he stood up and was suddenly face to face with Sarah.

"Want a drink?"

She had a beer in one hand and a glass of wine in the other. Luke smiled and reached for the beer.

"Cheers," Luke said, and they clinked glasses before taking long, slow drinks.

"Are you having a good time so far?" he asked, squinting against the sun. Sarah's sunglasses were wide on her face, the black tint so dark that he couldn't see through them into her eyes.

"It's fine. It's about what I expected." She gestured toward the lake and the lodge. "It's cute."

Luke wished he was wearing sunglasses so he could have rolled his eyes. Suddenly, he saw his mom trying to wheel a heavy cooler from the car to the picnic tables.

"I better go help her." Luke nodded toward his mother, relieved to be able to step away. Sarah seemed unbearable to have a conversation with. But then again, Luke admitted to himself as he jogged away, her smile was disarming, and every time she flashed it, he felt a pang of guilt in his stomach.

If he had been confused the past few days, now he was absolutely bewildered.

What is happening to me? he asked himself. *How can Mariah have gotten under my skin so much that I can't even talk to another woman without thinking I'm betraying her?*

As Luke helped his parents bring the last items from their car to the picnic shelter, he decided that, at this moment, there was only one thing he could do: Relax and just enjoy himself.

Wasn't that why he'd gone on vacation in the first place? Not to get involved in someone else's life. Not to stir up drama. And certainly not to become even more lost and confused than he'd felt the past week, ever since the company he'd poured his soul into for years turned its back on him like his dedication had meant nothing.

One bewildering situation was enough for him. He turned around and looked out at the lake, inhaling and exhaling slowly, grounding himself. His shoulders began to relax.

As the early-evening sun gradually descended toward the horizon, it cast a warm and enchanting glow across the lake and the rolling green hills. The heat from earlier had subsided slightly, and the air was now comfortably balmy, carrying the faint scent of freshly mowed grass. The branches of evergreen trees swayed gently in the soft breeze.

Feeling more relaxed and centered, Luke turned around and walked toward the picnic shelter to find that his parents had turned the ordinary structure into a summer dining wonderland.

The picnic table was covered in a mauve-colored tablecloth, with six beige bamboo placemats scattered around. In a straight line, three Mason jars were filled with water, and a single white carnation stood in each. A Bluetooth speaker filled the air with energetic classical music, and Luke felt like he'd been transported to a different world.

Soft-white string lights hung from the columns, illuminating the picnic table with a touch of sophistication. He watched as Sarah hung the final string on a nail and gently stepped down off the bench, holding the skirt of her dress close. Martha beamed as she thanked her for helping.

And all Luke could think about was how much he wished Mariah could see this. To see how an ordinary park picnic shelter could be turned into a beautiful space fit for what looked like a romantic garden party.

Then it hit him: This *was* a romantic garden party. Could his parents be doing all of this as part of their matchmaking scheme for him and Sarah? Ever since they'd gotten to the picnic area, his mother had been at Sarah's side, peppering her with questions and asking her help with decorating. Luke shuddered at the thought of all the embarrassing things his mom might be saying about him.

Shrugging off his misgivings, he had to admit that dinner was wonderful. Paul expertly grilled steaks and hamburgers, and the Dyers were impressed with the beautiful surroundings and the wonderful company.

Even Sarah seemed to have loosened up. Her cheeks were pink with a touch of sunburn, and she had kicked off her sandals and was walking around barefoot.

Luke sat at the picnic table, chatting with Mr. Dyer about his travels to Australia.

"When I worked at IBM, they sent me over there dozens of times," Mr. Dyer boasted. "It's a beautiful place. A few times I almost didn't come back."

Luke gave him a knowing nod.

"When do you think you'll go back over there?" Mr. Dyer said. "Your parents are always telling my wife and I about your career. It's fascinating."

"I may never go back there!" Luke said.

"Heavens, why not? Australia is a beautiful country."

"No, I mean work!" Luke's words slurred ever so slightly. He lifted his finger and pointed it upward in declaration. "I might just quit and never go back."

"Well, isn't that the dream!" Mr. Dyer laughed.

"It sure is, sir. Who needs the bother?"

Luke set down his empty beer can and stood up. "Excuse me."

Whoa, he thought, as he stood and found he was a bit wobbly. He decided to step away from the festivities and walk to the shoreline of the water. The lake air might do him some good.

He headed in the direction of a picnic table half hidden behind trees. It was only when he was a few steps away that Sarah was already sitting there, taking a slow drink from a can of beer.

"I wouldn't have pegged you for a beer drinker," he said as he approached.

Sarah looked up, a slight smile on her rosy-cheeked face.

"I drank all the wine." She laughed and rolled her eyes.

"How's your evening going?" Luke asked.

Sarah looked around and shrugged. "It's okay. I'm not really outdoorsy."

"Oh yeah? Then what's that?" Luke smiled and pointed to a fishing pole leaning against the picnic table.

"My mom bought it at a store on the drive here," Sarah said, looking toward the picnic shelter. "That's so not mine."

"Have you ever tried fishing?"

She just lifted an eyebrow and gave him a look. Luke laughed.

"Hope you don't mind if I take a look at it." He moved to the other side of the table next to her.

As Sarah drank the last of her beer and Luke fiddled with the fishing pole, the sun began to dip below the horizon. A gentle breeze rustled through the leaves of nearby trees, and a flock of ducks floated by slowly.

With a patient smile on his face, Luke prepared the fishing pole, a red and white bobber secured tightly toward the end. He'd been fishing countless times during his summers at Twin Pines, and it showed in his confident movements.

His eyes focused on a spot in the water where he believed fish might be lurking. Even though he didn't have any bait, he wanted to make sure the pole had a good cast.

In one fluid motion, he pulled his arm back, the fishing line winding around the reel. He paused for a moment, letting the tension build in the rod, and then with a flick of his wrist, he released the line. It sailed through the air, trailing a fine arc before it splashed down gently.

"That was a good one!" he said, a satisfied smile spreading across his handsome face.

He looked back toward Sarah, who was staring at him with a confused smile.

"What?" Luke said. "Did you miss it?"

"No, I saw it. I just...I just don't understand how that's *fun*. How can anyone have fun doing that?"

"Let me show you. There's no way you can understand the simple pleasure of fishing unless you try it."

"No, thank you. I'm not dressed for it."

"Come on," Luke urged gently. "It's not that hard. You might even enjoy it."

"That's not my style," Sarah protested again, but a smile was appearing on her face.

"You just said this whole place isn't your style...what's one more thing?"

Luke, lost in the magical feeling of the cool summer air and the sun glittering off the lake's crystal surface, held out his hand toward her.

"Come on. I'll show you."

Chapter 6

"That's it!" Jeffrey said with a dramatic sigh. "That's the last of it! I'm going home and never coming back!" He tossed a handful of wet, crumpled paper towels into the trash.

Mariah knew it had been a tough day for her friend. First, he'd been asked to work the concession stand. Everyone who worked at the lodge hated having to go down to the beach to work.

She especially knew how uncomfortable Jeffrey was working with the teenagers. He thought they all talked about him behind his back, gossiping about the forty-year-old guy working concessions. Mariah tried to reassure him that they had better gossip than him, but he couldn't be reasoned with.

Thankfully, he had returned to the lodge that afternoon soon after Mariah did. But as the day was winding down and they both agonizingly longed for the clock to move faster, he discovered that he'd left the door of the office refrigerator open.

For the past hour, they had worked together to clean up the mess, mopping up water and trying to determine which food might still be good. In the end, they just tossed everything.

Mariah was eager to get home, take off her work uniform, and relax outside with a novel. She'd just begun Ann Patchett's latest, and she couldn't stop thinking about it. That is, when she wasn't focused on helping Jeffrey with his problems. Or wondering if Luke had hopped in his fancy little blue sports car and was speeding toward New York City... with Sarah in the passenger's seat.

That image had been playing on repeat in Mariah's head all afternoon. To say she was still confused was a total understatement.

First of all, that kiss. Mariah had felt like a giddy teenager. She could still feel the stubble from his beard, which had grown quite a bit since he'd first arrived. She didn't even consider telling Jeffrey about the kiss. He would have laughed her right out of the park.

His scent had been overwhelming. She couldn't quite put her finger on it: a mixture of shampoo, the lake water, sunscreen, and spearmint. She could still smell it, just a little, in the air around her. Or maybe just in her mind. It was growing fainter, though, and she was eager to see him again.

If that's even going to happen, she thought to herself. *With whoever this Sarah is here at the park.*

"I'm going home, too!" Mariah said, turning off the lights in the back office and grabbing her purse. "But I *will* come back tomorrow."

"That's because Luke is still here," Jeffrey said, a smile growing on his face for the first time that afternoon.

"Maybe." Mariah rolled her eyes. "I don't know what I'm doing."

"I do! So go do it!"

Mariah laughed and hugged her friend.

What a beautiful evening, Mariah thought moments later as she got into her car and drove slowly down the hill away from the lodge.

The crimson hues of the setting sun painted the sky with a warm and inviting glow, casting long shadows over the lodge. The air was infused with the earthy scents of pine and wildflowers.

Mariah rolled down her windows to inhale the refreshing breeze, and she held her arm out the window, her skin soaking in the rays. Her other hand gripped the steering wheel lightly as she navigated the winding road, feeling her head clear for the first time since she'd left Luke on the path that afternoon.

She glanced in her rearview mirror and saw the lodge slowly receding into the distance. It stood as a silent sentinel, guarding the entire park.

She couldn't help but smile as the first stars of twilight twinkled overhead. The world seemed to slow down, and her cares began to melt away with the soft melodies of acoustic guitars from her favorite AM station filling the car.

When she got home, before she settled in for the night with her book, she'd do one thing: She'd pick out a nice outfit to take with her tomorrow. Luke had said he wanted to go on a real date with her. This time, she'd be ready.

As she rounded the edge of the lake toward the road that led out of the park, she smiled at the families still dotting the shorelines on blankets and at picnic tables. It really was a perfect summer night.

One table in particular caught her eye. A man and woman obviously smitten with each other were standing on the grassy shoreline. The woman was barefoot, and Mariah could see her gold sandals sparkling in the grass nearby. Her sundress was lovely, even if a bit too fancy for a day at the park.

The man stood behind her, so close that the front of his body blended with the back of hers. His arms wrapped snugly around her, and his hands sat on top of hers. She held a fishing pole awkwardly. Mariah watched as he guided it behind them, and then gently helped her cast. The red and white bobber landed in the water with a sharp splash.

The man whispered something in her ear, and she burst out laughing. Her head leaned back, causing her jet-black hair to nearly cover the man's face. As he sputtered and laughed and brushed the woman's hair off his face, he turned and looked to the right, just as Mariah drove by.

And even from that distance, she could see that it was Luke. Her blood ran cold, and she felt her heart drop into her stomach.

"I should have known!" she said, slamming her palms on the steering wheel. A split second passed before she realized she had come to a complete stop. Looking quickly in her rearview mirror, she saw another car slowly approaching.

Before she took off, she closed her eyes for half a second. When she opened them, she was looking toward the lake again. She had to make sure it was Luke that she'd seen.

This time, he was looking directly at her. Sarah was still nestled closely against him, but his hands were at his side. His mouth was wide open, and a look of fear spread across his face.

Mariah stared straight ahead and hit the accelerator, leaving the park and Luke in her rearview mirror.

~

"Come on, I need your help," Sarah laughed, as she clumsily tried to cast the fishing pole again. When she didn't receive a response from Luke, she turned around to look at him.

He was standing with his hands to his side and his back to Sarah. His body was stiff and unmoving, except for his head as it slowly turned to watch a car speed down the road and out of sight.

"Oh no," he mumbled. "Oh no, oh no."

"What is it?" Sarah said, a hint of annoyance in her tone.

He didn't say anything as he sat down at the picnic table. He rested his forehead in his hands and sighed loudly.

"What's wrong?" Sarah said again, walking a little unsteadily. When

Sarah put her hand on Luke's shoulder, he gently shook it off.

"I'm sorry," he said immediately, looking up at her. His face was pale and his eyes looked panicked.

"I didn't mean to... I think you're a great person, and tonight was fun. But..."

Sarah looked at him for a few seconds, her eyes wide and full of confusion.

"But what," she finally said, breaking the silence.

Luke didn't know how to answer. He had misjudged Sarah when he first met her. He hadn't expected them to get along as much as they had. His head began to pound and his eyes felt tired. What he couldn't say to Sarah was that he'd met someone and that he thought he might be falling for her.

He sat up straight, staring across the lake toward Twin Pines Lodge. A few lights peppered across its facade shone through the windows. It looked a little spooky in the dark.

I'm falling for Mariah, he thought to himself. He looked at Sarah, who was sitting across from him waiting for an answer.

"I'm just not ready." It wasn't a lie; it just wasn't the full truth. "Tonight was nice, though. Thank you." He turned to walk away as Sarah sat there, shaking her head and in disbelief.

Luke decided to call it a night and walk back to East Meadows Trail. It was probably a two-mile trek, but he needed the time and space away from anyone else.

Instead of walking the road that bordered the lake, Luke went the long way on a walking path that went into the woods and came out along a hill above the lake. His footsteps were heavy with guilt, a weight that seemed to grow heavier with each step.

He couldn't get Mariah's face out of his mind. He could see her through her open car window, the wind blowing her hair wildly around. It all felt like it was happening in slow motion: he noticed it was her driving by as he was reaching around Sarah's waist and laughing loudly at something she'd said.

Before he could undo anything, he had watched in disbelief as Mariah's face went from relaxed to alert as she thought she recognized him, to disbelief when she realized it *was* him.

His own face felt hot with embarrassment as he continued walking. When he reached the top of the hill, he sat down on a bench to catch his breath. It was the same one he'd rested on as a kid when he waited for a friend to catch up with him after pedaling his bicycle up the hill with all his might. Or waited on his father, who was running after him in a race.

He took a deep breath, the crisp night air filling his lungs. He felt the coolness of the bench beneath him, grounding him in the moment. But his guilt and confusion still gnawed at him, refusing to let go. He gazed out at the lake, its stillness mirroring the stillness he craved inside.

Earlier that day, Luke had felt good about how he and Mariah had left each other, standing just outside Twin Pines Lodge before Mariah had returned to work. At first, he'd immediately regretted bringing up Sarah and her family visiting the park. Mariah's face had changed, and he knew a seed of doubt had been planted.

But as he gently kissed Mariah's cheek and said what he could to assure her that he had eyes only for her, he felt lucky that the situation hadn't turned into something bigger.

Except that it had. His own stupidity and carelessness had ruined everything.

Luke's eyebrows were knitted closely together in frustration as despair slowly turned to confusion.

Ruined what? he said to himself. The same confusion he'd felt earlier in the week was creeping back into his mind. *What's there to ruin? In a few days, I'm leaving this place.*

In his professional life, Luke had been known for his decisiveness. He had what his superiors called a "bias for action." Even if he didn't know all the details or was unsure which decision to make, he made one anyway. In order to keep things moving.

But now, sitting alone on that bench atop the hill, he had no idea what move to make next. What to do to make things right with Mariah. They had never exchanged phone numbers. And even if they had, out here in the wilderness, cell phone service came and went.

As he sat there, staring out onto the hillside of grass before him, he began to notice something magical. It started with a single flicker of light, then another and another. Soon, the field was alive with the soft glow of fireflies. They danced in the twilight, their tiny lanterns creating a breathtaking display.

During his childhood summers at the park, Luke and his mom would catch fireflies most nights. He would hold a glass jar in his small hand, its lid punctured with tiny holes.

Fireflies, those mystical creatures of the night, would come alive in the warm summer air. His heart would race with excitement as he watched them flit and dart among the tall grass and wildflowers behind their cabin.

Every night, he embarked on a quest to capture as many as he could find. Each one added a tiny, radiant star to his glass jar. Then eventually, as the hour grew late, he released them back into the warm night.

Mesmerized by the fireflies now, Luke couldn't help but feel a sense of ease washing over him. They reminded him that there was hope, that he could find a way to make amends for his mistakes and find his path again. His path with Mariah.

With renewed determination, he stood up from the bench. First thing in the morning, he would head to the lodge and find Mariah.

Chapter 7

It took everything Mariah had to keep herself from slamming every door she encountered between the time she left the park and when she got home.

At Palmer's Market, she angrily grabbed a shopping cart, maneuvering it quickly through the aisles as she threw her items in it, not caring whether they got dented or broken. She had little patience for the slow walkers and long checkout lines, something she normally didn't give a second thought.

But tonight, she was fuming.

How *dare* Luke come to Twin Pines and act like a player. Not only was this her workplace but it was also her sanctuary, and he had disrespected it.

If I wanted this kind of drama, I'd move back to New York City and go back to the life I was living in my early twenties, Mariah thought.

When she pulled up to her house, she had to force herself not to slam the car door. As she stepped inside and removed her keys from the door handle lock, all she wanted to do was slam it so hard the glass from the small window at the top came crashing to the ground.

Instead, she softly closed it like she always did and carried the groceries into the kitchen. The house was quiet, and she didn't want to wake her dad in case he was sleeping.

As she flipped the light on, a voice startled her.

"Hey Mar!"

"Dad!" Mariah sat the bags on the counter. Her heart raced. "I thought you were asleep. You scared the heck out of me."

"Sorry, pumpkin. You sure were in your own world just now."

Tell me about it, Mariah thought.

"Rough day at work?"

"Not quite. Well, sort of."

Mariah's dad patted the chair next to him. "Have a seat."

"What are you doing up?" Mariah said as she sank into the chair. "I thought for sure you'd be asleep."

He smiled and looked out of the large bay window behind the kitchen table. In the corner of the backyard, a swing set from Mariah's childhood sat there, rusted and dirty.

As a kid, she and her friends would spend all day playing in that backyard, swinging high and making themselves dizzy running up and down the slide. From the swing set, she could see her parents sitting at the table or moving around the kitchen. Sometimes she saw them kiss. And while Mariah thought it was gross and especially when her friends saw it, too, it had given her a sense of comfort.

"It's a nice night," her father said. "Look at those stars. I bet it was just lovely on the lake."

Mariah sighed and rolled her eyes. She didn't want to think about what she saw on the lake. And what was probably still happening. And what might happen later, in someone's cabin.

"You okay? Boy, you look mad. Whoever did you wrong at work today better watch out." Her dad laughed and sipped his tea.

Mariah managed to smile halfway.

"I guess so. Sometimes you think you can trust someone, and then you realize you can't. That you never could."

Mariah's dad held the warm mug between his hands, a quizzical look on his face. "You're going to have to give me more than that. You're not talking about Jeffrey, are you?"

"Oh no!" Mariah said, her smile widening at the thought of her friend. "Jeffrey's my favorite person there. I don't know what I'd do without him."

"Is your boss giving you trouble?"

"No." Mariah hesitated, trying to figure out how to answer. "There's a visitor here this week that's being... a little difficult."

"Difficult how? The park crowd is usually as laid back as it gets."

"Not this one. He's a little high maintenance. He's from New York City, you know how visitors from the city can be."

Her dad chuckled.

"I bet it's his first time at the park, too. Maybe he didn't read the fine print and was surprised there's no running water in those cabins."

"Something like that." Mariah yawned and suddenly ached to be alone and burrowed deep under the covers of her warm bed.

"Cut him some slack, pumpkin. He may not even know he's being so difficult."

Mariah stood up and wished her father goodnight as she climbed the stairs to her bedroom. His words sat imprinted on her mind.

He had described Luke without even realizing it. As she climbed into bed and closed her eyes, the picture of him with his arms around Sarah played on repeat inside her mind.

One final thought danced around as she eventually drifted to sleep: If Luke just wanted to go on vacation and have a fling, that was his business, but it wasn't going to be with her.

~

When Mariah got to work the next morning, she slammed her purse on the registration desk. Jeffrey, startled, looked up from what he was doing and raised an eyebrow.

"I don't want to talk about it. And if Luke comes here looking for me, which I'm sure he won't, I don't want to know. And don't tell him where I am."

"Where, pray tell, will you be?"

"I have requested to work on the other side of the park today."

Jeffrey stepped off his stool, put his hands face-down on the desk, and leaned in closely toward Mariah.

"The *other* side?!"

The other side held the second entrance to the park, a lower-traffic, lesser-used area. But since some people tried to sneak in without paying the park fee, someone always had to be stationed at the welcome shelter there.

"That's right," Mariah said defiantly. *Where Luke would never go.*

Jeffrey looked concerned. "So what's really going on? You were all giddy yesterday evening when you left. What *possibly* could have happened?"

Mariah shook her head from side to side. She'd actually slept well last night, but now she was fuming again. She spent all morning with her incessant thoughts of Luke's betrayal, and right now, she wanted to set them aside and try to have a good day.

"Okay then," Jeffrey said when Mariah didn't answer. "I'll grab us something for lunch later and bring it *all* the way out there. Does that sound good?"

Mariah smiled, unable to reply. Not because she was angry, but because she had a lump in her throat. Jeffrey was so good to her. He was kind and made her laugh and supported her. Why couldn't everyone be like that?

~

In addition to the ability to pretty much go into exile, another benefit of working at the welcome shelter at the other side of the park was that it closed down at five o'clock. After that, visitors were allowed into the park for free.

Right at the top of the five-o'clock hour, Mariah began to shut down operations. She closed the window and made sure she'd picked up any trash from her lunch with Jeffrey. The last thing she needed was to get in trouble because a raccoon or black bear ravaged the little building.

She felt restless. She didn't want to go home, not just yet. It was times like this she wished she had a group of girlfriends she could meet up with, like she did when she lived in the city. She'd never worked to recreate those relationships here. And it was during times like this she regretted that.

As she exited the park and merged onto the highway, she thought about her options. A few miles down the road, the answer stood glistening against the mountains just off the highway at the next exit: the casino.

The evergreen-dotted mountains surrounding the huge casino reflected off the building's glass facade, creating dark spots across the modern, angular structure that seemed out of place surrounded by nature.

As Mariah pulled open the front door, an icy blast of air hit her squarely in the face and, despite how she was feeling, she smiled a little as she flashed her ID to the security guard and entered the casino floor.

She had always enjoyed the escape of the casino. When she entered the building, it felt like she wasn't in her hometown; it felt like she was in Las Vegas and far, far away. Which is exactly how she wanted to feel right now.

She navigated her way through the rows of slot machines, their screens flashing with animated graphics and spinning reels, inviting her to take a chance and try her luck. The constant chiming of winning machines added to the symphony of sounds, and Mariah could barely hear herself think: *Exactly* how she wanted it to be.

Mariah weaved through the crowd to the familiar corner of the casino where Kitty Glitter sat, her favorite slot machine. She plopped down on the soft, black leather stool and slid three twenty-dollar bills in. The familiar cat symbols began bouncing around the screen: fluffy white Persians, tabby cats, Calicos, and Siamese cats.

With each push of the "Bet" button to trigger her wager, Mariah relaxed into the ambience, excited at the prospect of her fortune changing.

"Are you having any luck?" a voice said beside her.

Startled, Mariah looked to her right. She didn't know how much time had passed; she'd been so immersed in the game that she had tuned out everything around her.

The man sitting at the machine next to her was in his mid-sixties and wearing khaki shorts and a Hawaiian button-down shirt covered in pink flamingos. He held a slot voucher in one hand and a drink the color of the flamingos on his shirt in the other. Despite being startled out of her daze, Mariah had to smile at him.

"Yeah, not bad so far." She pointed at the screen. "I've won ten dollars."

"You must be a lucky lady. I bet your husband thinks you're a lucky lady, too."

Mariah began to respond that she didn't have one, but thought better of it.

"Oh, he does. He'll be back any minute, and you can ask him all about it."

The flamingo shirt man stood to the side of her for a few more bets, and then he wished her good evening and continued strolling along the casino floor.

Mariah laughed and returned her focus to Kitty Glitter. She enthusiastically hit the "bet" button and watched as the spinning reels displayed the symbols Ace, King, Queen, and Jack, and of course, the bedazzled cats. She gently touched the screen to turn up the volume as dramatic sounds filled the space around her.

"Come on, bonus round!" she said enthusiastically.

The spinning reels came to a rest and she won one dollar and fifty cents, instead of the thousands of dollars one might think she'd won based on the loud, dramatic sounds coming from the machine.

As Mariah took a sip of her wine and began to slide another twenty-dollar bill in, she heard a voice behind her, this time a familiar one.

"Who was your friend?"

~

When Luke woke up, he felt rough. Definitely from the beers he drank the night before, but even more so from the look on Mariah's face that kept flashing across his mind as he struggled to fall asleep.

He'd gone to bed confident that finding her the next day at the lodge and taking her aside to explain the situation was the right thing to do.

But when he woke up, he didn't feel so certain. His stomach gurgled with nervousness, and his head throbbed with regret. At the first peek of sunshine finding its way through the trees and thin curtains, Luke popped an over-the-counter pain killer and rolled over, trying to get a few more hours of sleep.

Finally, he woke up around ten o'clock, feeling slightly better. His parents had left the cabin already, as he discovered when he wandered into the kitchen for coffee. A note next to the coffee pot read: *At the lodge having breakfast with the Dyers. Join us.*

Luke groaned. That was the last thing he wanted to do. He assumed Sarah was there, too, and there was no way he would risk Mariah seeing him with her again.

"How can I avoid everyone today?" he said out loud. "I just want to crawl in a hole and disappear."

After another cup of coffee and a light breakfast, Luke began to feel a little more alive. That's when he decided that he'd go for a long hike. It could get him out of the cabin and far, far away from everyone. Including Mariah. Because at this point, while he knew he needed to talk to her, he had no idea what to say or how to say it.

"Where's that map," he mumbled as he tossed around clothes and towels on his bed. After finally spotting it on the kitchen counter, he scanned it for a hiking trail that looked challenging enough to distract him from his racing thoughts. Three Sisters Trail looked perfect.

He changed clothes and packed snacks, water, bug spray, sunscreen, and the map. He also replied to his parents' note on the counter, letting them know that after his hike, he'd probably drive into town for a while and that he'd see them later that evening. The last thing Luke wanted was his parents worrying about him when he didn't come back right away this afternoon.

A half hour later, as the high noon sun rays beat down across the park and reflected off the lake, Luke stood at the head of Three Sisters Trail. The air was damp and warm, carrying the scent of pine.

With his backpack slung over his shoulder and hiking boots laced tightly, he knew this was exactly what he needed. He desperately hoped the renewal of the hike would help him find clarity and answers for what to do with the situation he'd created with Mariah... whatever that situation was.

He took his first steps onto the trail, leaves rustling underfoot and the distant calls of birds filling the sky. The past week had become a whirlwind of unexpected situations, both within his control and completely out of it.

The rollercoaster he was on with Mariah and whatever it was they were doing had actually been a distraction from the anxiety he'd felt from losing his job. But now that it had turned from a flirtation to something more serious, it felt heavy, like his job situation.

What the hell am I doing with her? he asked himself as his boots crunched over dried leaves and small twigs. He'd asked this question multiple times the past several days, but always, before he had time to sit and ponder an answer, he'd get swept up in her: seeing her bouncy, shiny hair from afar, the sparkle of her dark-brown eyes when she laughed, that light feeling he got when he anticipated seeing her at any moment.

And the mysteriousness of being so enthralled with someone he didn't really know at all.

He *had* been getting to know Mariah better, little by little, as she slowly allowed him in. Until he carelessly let himself be mesmerized by Sarah's beauty and charm and made the mistake of almost acting on it.

Luke shook his head, as if shaking away cobwebs. He picked up his pace, the trail meandering through the dense forest.

He didn't blame Sarah at all. From her perspective, he was probably ideal: single, successful, and living in the same city. And let's be honest, Luke thought, he wouldn't be surprised if she'd heard through the grapevine that he dated around. If she was looking for someone to have a little fun with, the Luke she thought she knew was perfect.

Except that he wasn't quite that person anymore. Something had shifted.

It started with the afternoon he got called into the CEO's office. Thinking he was being asked to give an update on the Thailand acquisition, Luke was a little annoyed at the late notice but grabbed what he needed. When he walked into her corner office and saw the head of human resources sitting beside her on the couch, Luke's stomach dropped.

The shift continued when he got home that evening. Sitting in his pristine, modern apartment, the silence making everything worse, he found himself calling his dad to see if they were still going to Twin Pines this summer. They were, in fact, his dad told him, and they were leaving in a few days.

Feeling almost like he was having an out-of-body experience, he heard himself say, "I'll meet you there on Saturday" before he hung up and fell asleep on the couch.

And now here he was, wandering the woods, feeling lost even though he had the map in his backpack, and wondering how he managed to get his heart involved in a situation.

Suddenly, Luke stopped walking and looked to his right, down into a ravine filled with broken tree limbs, ferns, and wildflowers. Boulders dotted the landscape, some jagged and sharp underneath the moss. At the steep bottom of the ravine, a thin creek snaked slowly through the wilderness.

As loud as he could, Luke screamed into the abyss.

"This was supposed to be a vacation!"

He stood there silently, his breath heavy and his voice echoing off the trees.

And just as suddenly as he had screamed, he began to laugh, loud and hard. And every time his scream replayed in his mind, he laughed even harder. Finally, he took off his backpack and sat down on the trail, trying to gain his composure so he wouldn't lose his balance.

Several hours later, with legs that felt like wet noodles and a backpack with nothing but empty food wrappers, Luke arrived back at the trailhead.

As he drove into town, his stomach growled. Glancing at the clock, he realized it was nearly dinnertime. It didn't take long to decide where to grab food, as he got off the highway exit: the casino buffet.

Chapter 8

Feeling like he wouldn't need to eat for days, Luke left the buffet and walked onto the casino floor. He hadn't gambled in years, and even then, he preferred messing around with penny machines.

When he was a kid on vacation at Twin Pines, he'd come to the buffet with his family. Afterwards, he'd go back to the park with his aunt and uncle, since he was too young to go out on the casino floor, while his parents spent the evening at the slot machines.

The casino had always felt like a mysterious and weird world full of sounds and cigarette smoke and lights, just across a carpeted line he wasn't allowed to cross.

As Luke slowly strolled the aisles between machines, he tried to find something that struck his fancy. What caught his eye was a machine with a giant white fluffy cat surrounded by diamonds, and sitting in front of it was a very familiar head of hair.

He stopped in his tracks, not sure whether to approach Mariah. Before he could decide, a white-haired man sat down on the stool beside her and pointed to her screen. As she turned to look at him, Luke caught a glimpse of her beautiful smile. The stranger said something to her, and her hair bounced as she laughed.

Luke's chest felt tight as a feeling of warmth and desire for Mariah fell over him. He wanted nothing more than to look into her eyes and see that smile. Before he knew it, the white-haired man stood up and walked away. Without giving it a second thought, Luke approached her.

"Who's your new friend?" he asked casually.

As Mariah's eyes met his, her expression was cold, and the air around them felt icy and heavy.

That wasn't what Luke had expected. He didn't know what he'd expected. Deep down, naively he thought maybe, just maybe, she'd forgotten a little about what happened.

Definitely not the case. Mariah didn't answer, and instead turned her attention back to the slot machine.

Luke's stomach twisted in knots, but he was determined. He hadn't expected to see her here, and he took this as a sign from the universe.

"May I sit down?" Luke gestured toward the empty seat in front of the machine beside her. When she didn't reply, he gently sat down.

Well I'm here, Luke thought. *Might as well play this machine a little, in case she doesn't respond to anything I say.*

"Where's your girlfriend?" Mariah said after several moments.

Luke had been fishing cash out of his wallet. His head jerked up. "What?"

"I said, where's your girlfriend?" Her eyes remained steely ahead of her, focused on the kittens bouncing all around the colorful screen.

Luke sighed. He slipped a crisp twenty-dollar bill into the slot machine. He looked over at her as it came to life with noises and lights.

"She isn't my girlfriend," he said at last. "I promise. But I guess I can see why you'd think that."

"You guess?"

"I suppose I deserve that," Luke said, smiling a little, trying to catch

Mariah's eye to see if he could discern just how mad she was. But she didn't turn her head a millimeter. She continued staring straight ahead, pushing the "bet" button a little too hard each time.

Luke sat on his stool, watching her play. After several minutes, he hit the "Bet" button on his own machine. Suddenly, the screen erupted in loud noises and fireworks.

"What the heck," Luke exclaimed, startled. He looked at Mariah. Her eyes, now wide with intrigue, look at his screen.

"You did a max bet! Did you mean to do that?"

"A what?!" Flustered, Luke looked at his screen and realized he'd wagered eight dollars instead of eighty-eight cents. And somehow he'd managed to hit the bonus on his first spin.

"Boy, aren't you lucky," Mariah said, her attention fully focused on his slot machine. Her face looked softer than it had a few moments ago, but there was still an icy edge to her voice.

"Yeah, I am." Luke looked at her, grateful she was talking to him again and almost forgetting about his bonus rounds waiting to be played. Mariah caught his wistful tone and she looked at him squarely. As their eyes lingered on each other for a moment too long, Luke could see her face relax ever so slightly.

"Well, what are you waiting for?" Mariah said almost teasingly. "Your fortune awaits."

Luke poised his finger over the "Bet" button. "Okay, here we go!" He ended up winning three-hundred dollars.

"Lady luck was on my side tonight!" Moments later he clutched the winning ticket tightly. Mariah stood up abruptly, straightened her purse on her shoulder, and grabbed her empty wine glass.

"I think I'm going to go home. Good night."

Luke was still staring at his winning ticket, and he looked up at Mariah, confused.

"What? Why?"

"Because... Because I don't know what I'm doing here. With all this." She gestured around her and sighed. "With you."

"Can we just talk?" Luke said. "Go home if you want, but please, I'd love to just talk. Even for a moment."

~

Mariah was glad for Luke's big win on the slot machine. Truly, she was. But at the mention of the word "lady," Mariah was suddenly thrown back into how she felt yesterday evening when she realized that she was "the other lady" that Luke was canoodling with this week. She felt her heart drop into her stomach. For a few moments, she'd gotten caught up in the fun of his win and had forgotten everything else.

Part of Mariah wanted to storm out of the casino and never talk to him again. Getting into a tangled love triangle was *not* in her plans, this summer or any summer. In fifteen minutes, she could be in her pajamas and snuggled under the covers.

But one look at Luke, sitting there on the stool looking wide-eyed with fear that she might do just that, might turn around and walk away and never come back, was all she needed to stay. *Just for a little bit*, she told herself. *Just to see what he possibly could have to say.*

"Let's see if we can find a quiet corner in this place," she finally said. Luke popped up and quickly fell into step beside her. After ten minutes of wandering through the maze of machines, waitresses, and security guards, they settle into a café table at the coffee shop just outside the hotel lobby.

Mariah stared at him as he fiddled with his winning slot machine voucher. He folded it carefully and put it inside the zippered pocket of his expensive-looking leather wallet. Finally, Mariah's impatience got the best of her.

"What are you doing here, Luke?"

He looked up at her, confused. "What do you mean?"

"I mean, did you follow me here?"

"No!" Luke's face flushed with embarrassment. "I didn't. I needed a place to get away from the cabin, my family. The park. Don't you ever just need to be alone?"

"Yeah, right, alone here with all these people." Mariah gestured around her. Her tone was tinged with sarcasm, but deep down she understood what he meant. Sometimes she wanted to be alone without being by herself. But she wasn't about to admit anything to Luke.

A waiter appeared at their table and sat down two mugs of tea. Mariah grabbed hers and wrapped her hands around it, the warmth bringing her a bit of comfort. Her stomach was a tangle of nerves and butterflies.

Several silent seconds went by. It was time for Luke to start speaking his mind. Finally, he leaned forward slightly, his voice soft. "You've barely looked at me since we sat down."

The casino coffee shop buzzed quietly around them: espresso machines hissing, chips clinking faintly in the distance. But at their little table, time felt stalled.

Mariah sat stiffly, her expression guarded.

"I know what you saw," he continued. "And I know what it looked like."

Mariah's jaw tightened. She didn't look up. "Then you know why I'm mad. And why I feel like I've been an idiot all week."

"Mariah..."

"I saw you with her. I know what it looks like when two people have a history."

Luke's voice was calm. "We do have a history. But not the kind you think."

Mariah looked up, eyes sharp. "What do you mean?"

"It's exactly what I told you yesterday. She's the daughter of family friends. My parents have a history with her parents, but I don't have a history with her. I barely know her."

"Could have fooled me."

Luke looked pleadingly at her.

"I had too many beers and got too comfortable." He leaned forward slightly, voice low. "Mariah, I didn't do anything. And I hate that I hurt you."

Silence stretched between them, thick and uneasy. Mariah looked down at her cup again and sighed.

"I guess there's more to this for me," she said quietly. "It's not just about what I saw. It's how fast my brain went there. How fast I decided you were just like everyone else that I cared about."

"Everyone else...?"

"My mom walked out on us. One day she was there, the next she wasn't. Just left a note. Said she couldn't stay married to someone who needed her so much." She paused, her voice tight. "My dad had gotten sick."

Luke's expression softened. "Mariah..."

She shook her head. "He's doing better now. But since then, I've kept everyone at arm's length. It's safer that way."

She sat still, her eyes fixed on the table. Slowly, her shoulders relaxed just enough to let air in. She began to feel as if a weight had been lifted.

Luke reached across the table, hesitating before placing his hand gently over hers. "I'm so sorry I made you feel that way."

She looked into his eyes. In them, she saw kindness and what she felt was the truth. And suddenly, she didn't feel the urge to run home anymore.

~

The tightness in Luke's chest finally loosened as Mariah visibly relaxed and seemed like her old self. She hadn't fully smiled—not yet—but the way she now leaned slightly toward him told him everything he needed to know.

She was still here; she hadn't walked away like he knew she really wanted to at first.

They left the coffee shop side by side, neither saying much. But the silence between them no longer felt tense or cold. It was a quiet rebuilding, a mutual catching of breath.

"Thank you," Luke said, breaking the stillness.

Mariah gave him a sideways glance. "For what?"

"For hearing me out. For believing in me."

She didn't answer, but gently reached out and gave his hand a small squeeze.

They were making their way toward the exit when Luke noticed people moving with purpose toward the side exit near the parking lot. Laughter and excited chatter hummed around them.

"What's going on?" Mariah asked, noticing it, too.

"Let's find out!"

The casino's side doors opened out into a warm summer night, the kind that clung to your skin and hummed with heat from the pavement. The scent of popcorn and fried food floated through the air. Luke blinked in surprise as he stepped onto the blacktop. He had forgotten how it felt to emerge from a dark casino into the sunlight.

The parking lot was packed with families. Bleachers had been set up at the far end, along with folding chairs and vendor carts. The mood was electric.

Luke caught the attention of a guy in front of him, who was holding a toddler on his hip. "Hey, what's happening out here?"

The man grinned. "Pop-up fireworks! They don't tell anyone the exact night, they just decide to do it when the weather's good."

Luke turned to Mariah, eyebrows raised. "Guess we're here on the right night."

She smiled—actually smiled this time—and the effect of it hit Luke like a sucker punch.

"Do you need to head out?" he asked hesitantly. "Maybe your dad needs you...."

"I'm sure he will, eventually. But not right this minute."

Luke felt his heart lift. They made their way closer to the edge of the parking lot where a low hill provided a decent view. They sat down on the grass, shoulder to shoulder. Around them, kids waved glow sticks and music played softly from speakers strung along the light poles.

It felt like summer at its most perfect.

As they waited for the show to begin, Luke stole glances at Mariah. The way her wavy hair moved slightly in the breeze, how her dark eyes reflected the string lights overhead. She wasn't leaning away from him anymore. If anything, he observed, she was leaning closer.

"You know," she said, glancing at him. "You kind of saved this night."

He tilted his head. "I was pretty sure I ruined it. The entire week."

"You almost did. But seriously," Mariah said, her voice softer. "Thank you for hearing me out, too. I don't talk about my family often. I know that was a little... intense."

Her expression grew thoughtful, and he could feel the weight of it settling into something new between them.

A loud crack snapped through the sky, and suddenly the night exploded in color. The crowd cheered as the first fireworks bloomed red, gold, and blue. The sound was thunderous, echoing off the walls of the casino behind them.

Luke suddenly realized something.

"This is our date," he said, looking into Mariah's eyes. "Sometimes the best things happen when there are no plans at all."

"Even though I'm in my work shirt again?" Mariah laughed, her eyes twinkling and her cheeks turning a rosy pink.

"I can't imagine you in anything else."

Mariah leaned into his side just slightly, her knee brushing his. Luke didn't move. He didn't speak. He just sat with her like that as the sky lit up again and again, bursts of color raining down like confetti.

She turned her face up toward the sky, her eyes wide with the kind of joy you can't fake.

"This is magic," she whispered.

Luke wasn't watching the fireworks. He was watching her.

"Yeah," he said. "It really is."

She turned to look at him, and there it was. That stillness, that pull between them like gravity had taken over. He didn't plan what happened next. He just leaned forward, the moment opening like a door.

And Mariah met him halfway, her lips soft against his, warm and certain.

The kiss felt like something they'd been building toward since the second they met. The fireworks cracked again above them, but for Luke, the world had gone quiet. All he could hear was the beat of his heart and the feeling of finally getting something right.

Chapter 9

Mariah exited the highway and merged onto the road that led into the park, her hands resting lightly on the steering wheel. She passed the large *Welcome to Twin Pines State Park* sign and waved at the woman sitting inside the welcome shelter.

The morning sun dappled through the thick canopy overhead and shadows danced across her dashboard. Her familiar drive through the park looked just the same as it always had: majestic trees lining the road and woodchucks darting across the road and into the thick brush.

It seemed like a normal morning, but today wasn't a workday for Mariah. She felt a small smile tug at the corners of her mouth as she approached the hill that led up to the lodge, and then drove right past it.

Her stomach flipped in a way that it hadn't for a long time until this week. Last night, as the final fireworks floated away, she'd shyly mentioned to Luke that she had the next day off. He didn't hesitate. He asked if she'd like to spend it with him.

Now here she was: not clocking in, not organizing checkouts or paperwork or managing guests. She was just at the park, able to enjoy it fully like so many others throughout the summer. And she had a surprise planned for Luke that she was sure he'd love.

Despite her excitement, something in the back of her mind left her feeling unsettled. As she approached the beach parking lot where she was to meet him, she finally faced what she'd tried pushing out of her mind all night and morning: today was Luke's last day at the park. Tomorrow, he'd check out from his cabin and leave. She turned her radio up a little and tried again to push the thought out of her mind.

She spotted Luke immediately. She shook her head slowly and laughed, caught off guard by how handsome he looked leaning against the side wall of the boat rental shack, his hands in his pockets. The sunlight made his hair sparkle, and his T-shirt clung to his shoulders just enough to make her heart thump a little faster.

He turned as she pulled her car next to the boat rental shack and rolled down her window.

"Nice shirt!" she yelled. The front of his light-gray T-shirt featured a raccoon roasting marshmallows around a campfire and the words Twin Pines State Park.

"I got it at the gift shop! That place is awesome!" Before Mariah had a chance to reply, Luke reached through her open car window and pulled her in for a hug. He smelled like musk-scented soap and coffee.

"Get in!"

Luke laughed, a little confused, but quickly got into the car. "Where are we going?"

"It's a surprise," Mariah stole a glance at him and smiled. "I'll give you a hint. You mentioned the other day how much you used to enjoy playing in this area of the park as a kid. Well, today we're going there to play."

"Glad I wore my sneakers!" Luke laughed and settled into the drive. His thick eyebrows knitted as he tried to figure out where they were going.

Mariah drove slowly toward the west side of the park. Luke leaned toward his open window, his eyes scanning the thick woods for deer, raccoon families, but most importantly, bears. Spotting a black bear in the park was a rite of passage for Twin Pines visitors, and even Mariah, who was at the park nearly every day, had only seen one a handful of times.

"Have you ever seen one?"

"Only once, probably twenty years ago," Luke replied, knowing exactly what she was talking about. "My mom and I were driving back from town. We were nearing the entrance to the park, I was just chatting away, and all of a sudden she grabs my arm and screams, 'bear!'

"It scared me to death," he laughed. "And I think I still have her handprint on my arm."

Mariah had been wondering about Luke's family, and so she took his story as an opportunity to try to learn a little more.

"Your mom sounds like a fun person." She turned her head slightly just in time to catch a glimpse of Luke's expression.

"I wouldn't say fun, exactly. She's a great person. A little high-strung, but a good person. She means well."

"That's all that matters." Mariah felt some relief knowing he was at least the type of person who got along with his mom. She'd once dated a guy who had forgotten to wish his mom a happy birthday. She broke up with him the next day.

"How about your dad?"

"What, is he fun?" Luke laughed. "Actually yeah, my dad is fun. It's been nice hanging out with him this week. You know, it's been nice hanging out with them both. I should do that more."

Mariah smiled as she continued driving through the thick forests of Twin Pines. Only a few cars had gone by, and no one had come up behind them. It was as if they had the park to themselves.

"Any brothers or sisters?"

Luke laughed. "Are you writing a report about my family?"

Mariah laughed and shook her head.

"I just tend to be curious about the boys that I let kiss me."

Luke leaned over and squeezed her hand, and Mariah's face flushed with happiness.

"No siblings," he said. "It's just me. I always wanted a sister though. What about you?"

"Only child, too. Just me and my dad. Unless you count Jeffrey, he's like a brother."

"That must be tough sometimes," Luke said, still holding lightly onto her hand. "With your dad not always being well."

"It can be. But I don't mind, not really." She never talked about her dad with anyone except Jeffrey, and even he didn't ask too often. She considered herself her father's friend and caretaker, and it didn't occur to her that it should be any other way.

A few quiet moments passed until Luke finally broke the silence.

"So where *are* we going?"

"You can't tell yet, Twin Pines legend?"

Luke laughed hard. "I'm a little rusty, I hate to admit."

"Luckily, we're here…" The turn signal clicked loudly as a wooden sign by a gravel road came into view.

"Thunder Rocks!" Luke exclaimed loudly.

~

Luke's heart filled with joy as Mariah drove her sedan gingerly along the windy gravel road that led up to the famous Thunder Rocks nestled inside of Twin Pines. Once parked, Luke practically jumped out of the car, reaching out for Mariah's hand as they sprinted toward the boulders.

As he approached, Luke closed his eyes briefly and inhaled the scent of the forest around them, birds chirping high in the tall, slender pines and the wind blowing leaves around them. Mariah was smiling big and her hair danced around her beautiful face.

Thunder Rocks was one of Twin Pines's most captivating natural landmarks. A labyrinth of ancient, building-sized boulders scattered across the forest floor, creating narrow alleys and natural sculptures that begged to be explored. When Luke was a kid, all he wanted to do was climb the giant boulders and pretend he was an explorer from millions of years ago, discovering new lands.

"It never gets old," Mariah said. She had followed him and was standing nearby, taking in the incredible scenery. "I haven't been up here in more than a year."

Luke registered surprise.

"If I lived nearby, I'd be here every day."

"You say that, but then your real job gets in the way, and a year goes by!"

Luke tilted his head back, his eyes tracing the jagged curve of the tallest rock in the clearing. The warm scent of moss and sunbaked sandstone surrounded them, heavy and earthy and grounding. Sunlight cut through the branches above, dappling the boulder with shifting patches of gold.

"I forgot how big this one is," he said, resting a palm against its cool surface. "When I was a kid, it felt like a skyscraper. We used to come here in the afternoons. My parents would pack juice boxes and peanut butter sandwiches, and I'd run around with a bunch of the other park kids. We used to pretend we were explorers or secret agents hiding out between the boulders. Playing hide and seek."

Mariah smiled faintly, her gaze still on the rock in front of them. "You ever win?"

He laughed softly. "Once or twice. But I also twisted my ankle here one summer trying to be a showoff."

Mariah stood beside him, her arms loosely crossed, her eyes climbing the jagged face of the tallest rock in the cluster.

"I only came here once as a kid," Mariah said thoughtfully.

"Just once? Really?"

Mariah nodded. "Yeah. My mom..." She paused and swallowed. "This was the only part of the park she ever liked. She said it felt magical. Said the rocks looked like sleeping giants."

Luke stayed quiet, listening to the squawking crows and rustling tree leaves, hoping Mariah would continue.

"I was maybe eight. She and I came up here one afternoon. I remember thinking she was different that day, she almost seemed happy. We sat on the tallest rock and watched the clouds move." She shook her head, eyes glassy.

Luke looked at the rocks again, suddenly aware of how much they'd both brought into this place, how it held pieces of their pasts from a place they shared all these years without knowing it. He turned toward her, as the sunlight filtered through the canopy, catching the edges of her hair like fire.

"Thanks for bringing me up here. This was so kind of you."

Mariah reached for his hand, and Luke took it easily, his fingers threading through hers like they belonged there. Just as they both belonged among the towering rocks of Twin Pines.

~

Mariah had one last surprise up her sleeve as she pulled back into the beach parking lot and turned off her car.

"I'm hungry. Let's have lunch. Grab that."

Luke laughed as he reached into the back seat and grabbed the cooler. They walked toward the boat rental shack to where the rowboats and canoes were tied up along the dock.

"Have you ever paddled one of these things?" she asked.

"Plenty of times. You forget who you're talking to?"

"Oh, right. Twin Pines legend," Mariah laughed.

She put the cooler into their tandem canoe, and then they both gently got in and pushed off from the dock. Small swirls of water from yesterday's adventures stood at the bottom of the canoe, soaking their shoes and socks immediately.

As they pushed off, the canoe wobbled slightly, and Luke overcorrected his paddle stroke. Mariah's sunglasses tumbled off her head and into the water. She grabbed them quickly before they began to sink.

"Relax," she said, laughing and shaking the water off her glasses. "You're not fighting a current."

Luke smiled sheepishly and settled into a rhythm alongside Mariah's. She could see the pink on his cheeks growing stronger, and she was torn between laughing and giving him a big hug.

Together, they glided across the lake's still surface. Dragonflies hovered like tiny helicopters, and the water looked like glass, mirroring the cotton-candy-shaped clouds above.

Mariah directed them toward a little cove tucked behind a small outcrop of trees, half-secluded and softly shaded.

"This was my secret spot when I worked boat rentals in high school and college. You can't hear anything but the birds here."

Once ashore, Luke laid out the blanket. Mariah unpacked ham sandwiches, apples, and peanut butter cookies she'd made that morning. Her father couldn't believe it when he'd wandered into the kitchen and seen her baking.

"I wasn't sure what you liked," she said as she handed Luke his food.

He gave her a grateful look. "This is the best lunch I've ever had." Mariah looked up at him, and they both immediately burst out laughing.

They sat together, legs stretched out, the water gently lapping the shore beside them. Time moved slower there, like the park bent the clock slightly to let people catch up to their own lives. The breeze rustled the leaves above them, and a heron lifted from the far end of the lake, wings wide and slow.

Despite the peaceful, beautiful day, Mariah felt the familiar twinge of anxiety in the bottom of her stomach, churning so much she couldn't really enjoy her lunch. She knew she needed to say something, but she couldn't figure out how. Luke must have noticed how silent she'd become.

"What's going on over there?"

Mariah looked up from her sandwich to see him smiling at her.

"Nothing…" she lied. She sighed softly. "I talk so much when I'm at work that sometimes I like to enjoy the silence around me." That part wasn't a lie.

"That I can understand," said Luke as he bit loudly into his apple.

After five minutes, Mariah decided to just pull off the band-aid. "You're leaving in the morning, aren't you?"

~

Luke was having an incredible day with Mariah. First the surprise trip to Thunder Rocks, now lunch on the lake. This is the date he'd wanted with her, not stolen moments in the lodge or random run-ins in town. He'd be lying, though, if he said the same question she'd just asked hadn't been nagging at him all morning, too.

The breeze off the lake rustled the edge of the picnic blanket, and a bird called out from the trees behind them, long and lilting, like it had nowhere else to be.

"Yeah," he said finally, the word settling in the space between them.

"I'm leaving in the morning."

Mariah nodded slowly, like she'd already prepared herself to hear it. But there was something in her expression he couldn't ignore, an ache just beneath the surface.

He leaned back on his elbows, staring up at the tree canopy. Light filtered through the leaves, casting soft patterns across the blanket. It was so still, so peaceful.

"I keep thinking about the drive," he said after a while. "And what I'm actually driving back to. Everything seems so out of place."

Mariah's brows knitted as she listened closely.

He paused, swallowing the knot in his throat. "It's a weird thing. I've always had a plan. After college was grad school. Then join a firm and climb the ladder. Get to travel around the world. I've done all that, and I'd planned to do more."

Luke looked into Mariah's eyes, which were filled with worry and questions. "I'm going back to an empty apartment in a city that doesn't care if I show up or not." He realized how doom and gloom he'd suddenly become. He laughed lightly to cut the seriousness of the moment.

"Maybe I'll get a cat!" He looked over at Mariah, who was still staring at him with concern.

"But here..." He gestured vaguely around. "Here, I feel like a person again. I feel like myself, even though I've lost a little of who I am. And now I'm supposed to leave this place. And I don't know what I'm walking into, or if I even want to go."

Mariah's eyes were wide and her cheeks flushed.

"What are you saying?" she finally asked.

Luke suddenly felt silly. This date was meant to be fun, but instead he, yet again, was using Mariah as a confessional to unload the burdens. He shook his head.

"Never mind me. Let's make the most of this day. I have another hour before I need to meet up with my parents. They want to spend the rest of the day with me, since they don't know when they'll see me again."

Mariah's right eyebrow shot up. Luke knew what she was going to say.

"No, I haven't told them yet..."

"You should consider doing that," Mariah said gently, as she stood to shake out the picnic blanket and tuck it back into her bag.

He knew she was trying to help. But he didn't want to mention anything to his parents until he'd be able to answer all the questions he knew they'd have. Especially his mom. And right now, he was more confused and lost than ever about that part of his life.

In fact, as of that moment, the only thing he was certain of was his feelings for the woman standing in front of him.

Chapter 10

Mariah stared at the ceiling, the pale morning light casting a soft glow across her bedroom walls. Her alarm hadn't even gone off yet, but sleep had long since evaded her. Her body ached with exhaustion, and a little bit of sunburn from yesterday, but her mind was still running at full speed, replaying every conversation, every touch, every quiet look between her and Luke.

It had only been a week. Seven days, maybe less. And somehow her world had tilted on its axis.

She sat up slowly, swinging her legs over the side of the bed. Part of her wanted to laugh. Just a week ago, Luke hadn't existed in her orbit. Now? His name sat somewhere between her ribs and her throat, impossible to ignore. The past two days had been... God, had they actually been real? The fireworks. That kiss. His hands on her waist. The way he listened when she spoke. Thunder Rocks, lunch on the lake.

She rested her elbows on her knees, pressing her hands to her face. Her heart felt full and tight. Then she stood up and crossed to her bedroom window that overlooked the backyard. Outside, the sunlight was just beginning to kiss the tops of the pines.

Luke was leaving today. Back to the city a life he wasn't sure about.

She wanted to believe that what they'd shared meant something, that it was real and not just something to pass the time because Luke was bored and lost.

But her mother had once told her that love didn't always mean roots. And Mariah had never forgotten the way it felt when someone important walked away. She hated gray areas. She'd spent too much of her teenage years wondering whether people were coming back, only to learn that most didn't.

Despite this, somehow, Mariah felt a tingling growing in her stomach, a flutter that reminded her that hope was still alive within her. She began to feel better as the morning progressed.

By the time she arrived at the park, she practically floated up the stairs to the restaurant like her sneakers had traded their soles for helium. The morning sun poured in through the lodge windows, making the wood paneling glow golden. It was a busy morning: visitors had begun checking out, and a delivery truck was beeping somewhere near the maintenance shed.

Jeffrey was already upstairs at their usual table near the window. Mariah had texted him last night and asked if he could get to work a little early so they could catch up.

"Oh, she arrives," he said as Mariah approached, dramatically sitting his drink down. "And she's glowing like she just floated down from Heaven... or possibly Luke's cabin. Tell me everything, and do not hold back."

Mariah laughed and slid into the chair across from him. "Calm down."

"Absolutely not. The last time I saw you, you were ready to report him to the authorities for emotional whiplash, and now you're out here looking like a romance movie poster. What happened?"

Mariah clasped her hands on the table, grinning. She told Jeffrey everything: Luke appearing at the casino and the conversation that followed. She shyly described the kiss, then their day spent together yesterday.

Jeffrey blinked. "You're telling me the most romantic clichés in history actually happened to you in real life?"

Mariah giggled, looking around to make sure no one was watching. "It was perfect. I don't even care if it sounds silly. It just felt right."

Jeffrey sat back in his chair, still grinning, but a little more thoughtful now. "Okay, so let me gently play devil's advocate here."

"Uh oh."

"Don't worry, I'm still rooting for him. But you've known him for, what, six days?"

Mariah made a face. "Basically." She threw a crumpled napkin at him.

"I'm just saying," Jeffrey continued, his voice softer. "I don't want you to get swept up so fast that you miss something important. Like, do I love that he watched fireworks with you instead of running off with mystery-woman Sarah? Yes. Do I want to make sure he's not secretly a drifter with three identities? Also yes."

Mariah leaned back, exhaling. "I know. It's crazy. All of it."

"But you like him?"

She nodded. "A lot."

"Okay then. Just promise me you'll keep your eyes open. And maybe don't start naming your future children yet."

"I already ruled out 'Fannie' and 'Ferdinand' just in case," she teased.

Jeffrey cackled. "You are not okay."

Mariah felt it again: that warmth in her chest that had nothing to do with Luke or the hot coffee in her mug and everything to do with being known. This was the best part about Jeffrey: he could call her out and still be fully in her corner.

After a pause, he added: "Seriously though, Mariah, I'm happy for you. Most of the summer, you've seemed... heavier. This thing with Luke has put some lightness back in your step, even when some drama gets sprinkled on top."

She didn't say anything right away. Just smiled into her mug and let the morning sun do its best to hide the tears that were suddenly way too close to the surface.

"Thanks," she finally said quietly.

They sat for a few more minutes, watching a canoe drift slowly across the lake. Then Jeffrey broke the moment.

"If he hurts you, I'll replace all his shampoo with mayonnaise."

Mariah snorted. "I fully support that."

Jeffrey looked at his phone and groaned. "Alright, lovebird. Let's get to work."

Before they could stand up from their seats, the door to the restaurant creaked open and two women stepped in. Mariah froze. It was the dress she noticed first: that silky summer dress she had seen from a distance, fluttering in the breeze next to Luke as he held another woman in his arms.

Jeffrey noticed Mariah had stopped moving. "What's... ?"

"That's her," Mariah said quietly, nodding toward the pair.

Jeffrey turned casually to look. "And apparently her mother. They look like they were made from the same 3D printer, just twenty years apart."

Mariah stifled a laugh and composed herself as Sarah and her mother wandered toward the empty table next to them. She tried to calm the rumbling in her stomach.

Remember, you have nothing against this person, she thought. This person she'd spent so much time and energy thinking and talking about, who didn't even know she existed.

What a weird week, she thought for the millionth time.

Sarah dropped her purse onto the table and sat down, crossing her pale legs and knocking a piece of grass off of her gold sandal.

"This place is a dump. It smells like a musty attic in here, the park has, like, zero cell phone service, and don't even get me started on the town. The entire downtown is five buildings."

"Is it really that bad, dear?" her mom asked, half rolling her eyes but clearly amused.

"I just don't get how people live like this," Sarah added.

Jeffrey blinked. His expression was so dramatically stunned it would've made her laugh if her stomach hadn't just dropped to her shoes.

Sarah's mother slipped her sunglasses onto her head and picked up the laminated menu with two manicured fingers, as though afraid it might stain her hands. Sarah rolled her eyes and leaned back in her chair.

"I can't believe Luke used to come here every summer."

Mariah's head tilted, her eyebrows shooting up at the sound of his name.

Sarah's mother leaned in a little. "Speaking of Luke, you haven't said a word about him since the cookout."

Sarah smiled slowly, like she'd been waiting for someone to ask. "Honestly? I think he's amazing."

Her mother raised her eyebrows. "Really?"

"He's handsome and charming." Sarah stirred her iced tea, and, with her other hand, counted on her fingers as she listed Luke's attributes. "He's incredibly successful, with an apartment on the Upper East Side."

Her mother tilted her head. "But I thought you said he brushed you off at the lake the night of the cookout."

Sarah waved a hand. "Did I? I must have overreacted. I think he's in this weird nostalgia bubble right now. You know how some guys get sentimental about trees and childhood summers and campfire songs. This place is sacred to him or something."

Sarah glanced out the window toward the lake. "But once he's back in the city, to his real life, he'll remember who he is. And we'll have more opportunities to get to know each other. We already talked about having dinner once we both got back."

Mariah stood up slowly, pushing away her empty coffee cup, a confused look on her face. Jeffrey didn't speak.

"I—" Mariah started, then stopped. She motioned quietly for Jeffrey to follow her. As they raced down the stairs, she spoke quickly.

"That sounded like someone who thinks she still has a shot with Luke. I wonder where she got that idea?"

Her glow from this morning felt like it had been rained on and stomped out.

After a beat, Jeffrey leaned in. "Take a deep breath. This doesn't mean Luke is lying. Sarah could be misreading the situation."

Suddenly, Mariah went from feeling like her stomach had dropped to her knees to feeling like fire and brimstone was coming out of her ears.

Even if Sarah was misreading the situation, it didn't matter anymore. Not to Mariah. She actively moved in ways to avoid drama in her life, and now she was somehow involved in a love triangle out of nowhere. Despite the highs from their time spent together this week, she thought back on the misunderstandings and how they all centered around this other woman.

She had to speak to Luke right now, before he left. Before it was too late.

~

Luke couldn't remember the last time he'd slept so well.

Even waking up early hadn't bothered him, not when the morning sunlight cut across his cabin like golden ribbon, and not when he found himself grinning like a fool the second he remembered why he felt so good.

Their day at Thunder Rocks. The way she looked up at the fireworks and whispered, "This is magic." The kiss. And the part that had struck him most, the part he hadn't been able to shake, was how right it all felt.

His parents had left early to meet the Dyers for breakfast at the lodge restaurant one last time before they left for home. He knew it was rude to decline the invitation to join them. But he was afraid it would be awkward between him and Sarah, and he knew his ever vigilant and observant mother would pick up on the tension instantly. And he didn't even want to think about upsetting Mariah again, even though he knew she trusted him.

So he pretended he was asleep while his parents got ready. After he heard the crunch of their shoes walking down the gravel driveway, he got up and made coffee. After doing some packing to prepare for departure later that morning, he decided he needed to lace up his hiking boots and get outside one more time. He didn't know when he'd be at the park again, and being surrounded by a familiar and comforting forest was what he needed before his journey back to whatever awaited him in New York City.

Echo Rim Trail was a moderate two-mile hike and one of Luke's favorites. It wound high behind the lodge before dipping down into a few quiet switchbacks filled with ferns and moss and the occasional bright orange mushrooms.

Later that morning, with no one else on the trail, it was just him, salamanders, and his thoughts of Mariah. Yesterday they'd been afraid to talk in real detail about his departure from the park, hinting at it but not actually making any plans for next steps.

He decided that when he went to the lodge one final time to turn in the cabin key, he'd get her phone number. With the lack of cell service in the park, they still hadn't exchanged numbers. He loved how old school it felt. Mariah had been right that first day they met: not much had changed since he'd been there as a kid.

An hour later, sweaty and chugging the last of his water, Luke slowly walked the final curve of the hike and spotted the gravel trailhead through the trees. He dug his car keys out of his backpack as the glittery blue of his car showed through the foliage.

"What the…" he said out loud as the trailhead came into full view. Parked two spots over from him was a familiar, dusty Honda Accord. And there Mariah was, leaning against the driver's side door, arms crossed, one ankle tucked behind the other like she'd been there for a while.

Luke felt excitement in his stomach, and despite feeling fatigued from his hike, he picked up his pace and practically sprinted toward the cars.

"Hey there!" he yelled, lifting his arm in an excited wave as he approached her. "You following me?" Smiling at his joke, Luke leaned in for a hug, but something made him pause.

Mariah wasn't smiling. Instead, she mumbled a quiet "hello" and put her hands deep in the pockets of her shorts.

"What's going on?" Luke said, reaching out and gently touching her arm. To his surprise, she flinched slightly and took a small step back.

"We need to talk. I overheard Sarah this morning talking about you. At the restaurant."

And just like that, the morning turned. A little of the joy that had been holding court inside his chest all morning flickered like one of his dad's campfires. He barely had time to process the words "I overheard Sarah" before Mariah stepped forward, her voice steadier.

"She was sitting in the restaurant with her mom near my table. I wasn't trying to listen, but it was hard not to when she started talking loudly about the park."

Luke frowned. "What did she say?"

Mariah made a sweeping gesture with her hand. "The park is disgusting, she doesn't understand why people want to spend so much time here, she can't believe you used to come here every year, and she hopes she never has to come back."

Luke felt a sting, as if Sarah had insulted him personally.

"I was getting ready to walk away, and then she started talking about you."

Luke held his breath as Mariah continued.

"She said she thinks you're just playing hard to get. That the night by the lake meant something. Once you're both back in the city, you'll come to your senses. And she can't wait to start dating you."

Luke felt his stomach twist. "Mariah—"

"She talked like it was inevitable."

"I haven't encouraged her, I haven't—"

"But it sounds like you didn't shut it down, either," Mariah cut in.

"I didn't even know she was *that* interested until you just told me!"

Mariah didn't let up. "You must have left space for her to keep believing in something. Why would she say all that?"

"I don't know, Mariah. I told you everything about what happened that night by the lake. And I also told you that it meant nothing to me. That hasn't changed."

She sighed and shook her head. "You know I'm not the type of person to let myself get strung along by someone who can't figure out what he wants."

Luke ran a hand through his hair, suddenly aware of the sweat on the back of his neck. "That's not fair. I do know what I want... I want you."

"Well, Sarah thinks you want her."

"I haven't been leading her on, Mariah." Luke's voice was stern. "I've been here. With you. Every moment I could be. You think I have feelings for her? I'd never even met her until earlier this week."

Mariah froze, and before Luke could take back what he said, she stopped him.

"And you could say the same thing about me."

He looked at her pleadingly, unsure of what to say.

"It's different with you," he finally said, feeling tired.

"How? How is it different?"

But Luke suddenly felt exhausted. The emotional rollercoaster of the last week finally caught up with him, and his shoulders slumped. He stood against his car, silent.

Finally, Mariah spoke. "I shouldn't have let this go so far." She stood there for a moment, hesitating to speak, as if she couldn't believe those words had escaped her. She composed herself and continued.

"This isn't just a summer fling for me. This is my home. My job. My whole life's tied up in this place. And right now I feel like I'm gambling with all of it."

Luke's face went still. He was still feeling confused by the anger coming from Mariah, but this comment turned his confusion quickly into irritation. Feeling some energy coming back into his body, he paused before speaking, then finally, he shook his head and looked at her.

"Oh. So that's what this is."

"What?"

"You think your life's more important than mine. And I'm a... a loser who can't be worth much because he can't keep a job."

Mariah blinked, her head moving slightly back as if a gnat had flown too close to her face. "That's not what I meant—"

"It's not?" Luke said, his voice shaking slightly. "You just needed a reason to believe this wasn't going to work, and Sarah gave it to you on a silver platter."

Mariah's jaw clenched ever so slightly. Luke felt the anger rumbling inside, and he spoke suddenly with sheer emotion.

"Maybe getting to know Sarah when I get back to the city isn't such a bad idea. The only thing you and I have in common is this place." He waved his hand around, gesturing toward the tall evergreens looming over them like statues.

With that, Luke could see Mariah's eyes grow bright with tears. He felt his chest tighten but he had made up his mind. He turned and opened the car door, but before he climbed in, he glanced back one last time.

"You know, I don't even know why I came back here. I should've stayed away like I've been doing for years."

Mariah opened her mouth like she wanted to say something else, something softer.

"Maybe you should have," Mariah said instead, almost too quietly for Luke to hear. But he had.

Luke slammed the door shut, threw the car into reverse, and peeled out of the gravel lot, tires spitting dust as he sped away from the trail, from Mariah, from the one thing that, until ten minutes ago, had felt like it might actually be real.

Chapter 11

Luke's car kicked up dust in a fast, sharp cloud as he turned out of the trailhead and disappeared down the road.

Mariah stood beside her car, motionless, eyes narrowed against the grit in the wind. She had imagined a lot of endings when she was driving to find him that morning, but certainly not this one.

Suddenly remembering she needed to get back to the lodge, she looked down at her watch. It was Saturday morning, when guests would begin checking out from their week-long cabin stays.

Mariah drove with the car windows down and the already warm morning breeze blowing her hair in her face. She didn't bother to push it away or tie it back. She felt numb. By the time she pulled into a staff parking space and hurriedly walked in through a side entrance, she felt like someone had replaced her bones with stone.

The lodge was filled with the low thrum of departure-day energy: kids chasing each other down the hallways, dads taking one more selfie in front of the giant taxidermy bear in the museum, moms taking the little ones into the restrooms for one more break before hitting the road.

She took a deep breath and stepped behind the front desk. On the stool next to her wasn't Jeffrey in his usual place. Instead it was Samantha, the seasonal college student. Samantha was normally a lifeguard at the swimming pool near the campground, but the pool had been closed for repairs all month. Jeffrey had driven across the park to work at the entrance on the other side.

As much as she loved Jeffrey, Mariah was relieved. He would have taken one look at her and known something was wrong. And she was too overwhelmed with anger and embarrassment to explain anything.

She smoothed her hands over her legs, grounding herself. But her gaze drifted toward the front windows as she heard a familiar sound: the unmistakable clank of the first keys of the morning hitting the bottom of the wooden box just outside the front doors. Soon the box held enough keys that the sound changed: not the hollow, lonely clink anymore, but the muted tack-tack of plastic and brass rubbing against each other.

The sound normally brought Mariah a quiet kind of satisfaction. It was the park's version of applause: a soft, metallic signal that a family had finished a week of hiking trails, making s'mores, spotting deer at dusk, and maybe, if they were lucky, spotting a black bear cub. Each key had a life behind it.

But now, every clink rattled her nerves. And all the while, in the back of her mind, were questions: Will Luke come in? Just to say goodbye, to see her, to… fix the wrong way they'd left their last conversation?

Mariah shook her head and told herself she didn't care. She'd already said she had wished he'd never visited the park this summer. And she'd meant it.

Hadn't I? she asked herself. Her eyes kept drifting to the windows.

An hour later, something outside caught her eye. A deep, sparkly blue shimmered beneath the sun. The familiar curve of a hood and the slope of a windshield. Mariah sat up straighter, her spine stiff against the back of the wooden stool. Her eyes locked onto the car as it eased into the parking spot closest to the lodge's front doors.

It was definitely Luke's. Her pulse surged as she stared out the window.

The driver's side door opened, and there he was: tall, broad-shouldered, walking toward the building like he hadn't shattered her that morning at the trailhead. Her eyes flicked between the wide front windows and the double doors of the lodge. He wouldn't come in. Would he?

Everything in the room around her fell away. The ambient hum of the vending machines. The quiet shuffle of flip-flops on the wooden floors. The copy machine at the back of the office.

She watched the lodge doors and waited. He was so close. Then, Mariah heard the sound. The clank of a key hitting the top of a pile of identical keys. She didn't need to look out the window again. Somehow, she just knew it was his.

Still, her eyes followed on instinct. She caught the glint of sun on his windshield, the slow reverse, the flash of his taillights.

And then he was gone. Gone, just like she told him to be.

~

Cabin fifteen on East Meadows Trail felt too quiet without Luke's parents there. They'd left a few hours earlier, their SUV packed tight and his mom already talking about what needed to be defrosted for dinner. Luke had offered to stay behind and finish the cleanup: sweep the dusty floor and porch, drop off the trash at the refuse center, clean out the fridge, double-check for anything they might've left behind.

It wasn't about being helpful. He just didn't want to be around anyone. And, if he was being honest with himself, some small, desperate corner of him hoped Mariah might show up.

The silence inside the cabin was thick. His duffel bag sat by the door, packed down to the last pair of dirty socks. All that remained was the faint, earthy scent of the woods creeping in through the window screens and the midday squawks of birds.

Luke reached for the cabin key on the table and held it in his palm for a moment before closing his fist around it.

He opened the door slowly and stepped out onto the porch, letting his eyes drift across the green-painted siding, the flaking trim, the metal "15" bolted to the porch post. He stood there longer than he meant to, staring like the place might blink back at him, like it could offer answers.

Finally, he pulled the door shut with a soft click, let the screen door slam behind him, walked down the porch steps, and loaded his things into his car.

The drive to the lodge was short. The road twisted gently through the park, past slow stretches of the lake where paddleboats drifted, carrying couples who wanted to get some time on the water before the sun was too hot that afternoon. The air was warm but thick with moisture, the kind that clung to your skin and curled the edge of every leaf. Wildflowers along the roadside had begun to droop, desperate for even the lightest rain shower.

Tall pines lined the edge of the road, and their shadows flickered across the windshield as Luke drove beneath them. He remembered riding along it in the back seat of his parents' station wagon as a kid, forehead pressed to the glass, trying to count deer in the woods. Now it felt like it was moving him backward and forward at the same time, pulling him out of something he hadn't been ready to leave.

A group of kids rode by on bikes, their tires crunching over gravel, hair flying in all directions. They laughed like nothing in the world could ever go wrong.

He pulled into the front lot of the lodge, eased into the spot closest to the doors, and killed the engine. The building stood there, unchanged. But Luke wasn't the same man who'd driven toward it a week ago.

His hands stayed on the steering wheel for a moment longer, fingers tightening once, then loosening.

He looked at the doors. He could walk in. He could look for her. He imagined the front desk, the creak of the floor in front of it. He pictured Mariah sitting there, in her green polo shirt and her wavy hair looking wild around her beautiful face.

He could say a real goodbye. One that didn't end in anger. Instead, he stepped out of the car and approached the key return box. Pausing for a moment, he looked toward the front doors, then let the key drop.

~

Six hours later, the familiar buzz of his keycard activated the front door lock with a green light and a soft beep. Luke stepped inside his apartment, the weight of his duffel bag dragging against his shoulder.

The cleaning service had come while he was gone. The white marble counters gleamed, the beige sofa pillows were fluffed. The scent of something lemony clung faintly to the air. Everything was in its place.

He took a few steps forward. His chest tightened. In his mind, he tried to pull himself back to the soft rustling of the forest at dusk, the musty scent of pine needles. He closed his eyes and imagined the ripples of lake water against the beach and the feel of the cold water across his body as he dove from the pier like he did when he was a kid.

Suddenly, his senses were overtaken by the smell of Mariah's strawberry shampoo in the breeze when she turned her head toward him. The heat of her body as she sat close to him that night at the casino, the fireworks cracking loud and flashing high.

Luke sank down onto the edge of the couch, elbows on his knees, and stared at the carpeted floor like he might find something there that made sense.

~

The last two days had been brutal and today was no different. Mariah's heart and mind were still knotted from the morning Luke had left, but now a thick layer of fatigue had settled on top. She'd barely slept last night. Every time she closed her eyes, all she could see was him walking away from her forever.

Still, when the morning came, she showed up to work. And when someone called out sick, she agreed to cover the evening shift, because that's what she did. Now, she regretted that decision with her whole being.

The clock crawled toward nine o'clock, and Mariah handed the last of the day's paperwork off to the overnight attendant. She didn't even try to muster a "goodnight."

Outside, the air had cooled. The sky had deepened to a soft, dark blue. Crickets sang along the edges of the parking lot, and the warm scent of cedar drifted from the trees. She climbed into her car and began the familiar drive away from the lodge. The night air slipped through her cracked window, warm against her cheek.

Even now, with her heart bruised and exhausted, the lake calmed her. It always had. She drove beneath the sky that was beginning to pepper with stars.

"I belong here," she said out loud, with a certainty that had nothing to do with Luke and everything to do with herself.

She was halfway across the narrow road that curved gently along the top of the dam when bright, sharp headlights appeared ahead. Her first instinct was dread. A guest in trouble? A cabin issue?

"Not tonight," she groaned, as the other car dimmed its brights and slowed.

She eased her foot off the gas. Maybe there was an animal in the road. She crept forward, matching the other car's crawl. A soft breeze stirred the tall grasses along the dam, and in the shadows, a heron fluttered across the surface of the lake. As the two vehicles inched past one another, she glanced to her left.

Her heart slammed against her ribs as her eyes locked with Luke, and she hit the brakes. Luke's car stopped, too.

There he was, lit by moonlight and dashboard glow, a stunned and unmistakable smile spreading across his face.

Throwing the car into park and leaving the engine running, Mariah jumped out. The air around her pulsed with the sounds of frogs and the faint rush of water from the spillway below, but all she could hear was her own heartbeat.

The wind rustled the treetops above them like a soft hush, like the forest itself was watching, waiting. Before she could reach him, Luke was already there.

Mariah felt herself being lifted into the air and twirled around in his strong embrace. He wrapped his arms around her like he'd never let go. Exactly like she'd always imagined.

As she spun in circles with him, a laugh escaped her that quickly broke into a half-sob. Fireflies blinked around them like tiny lanterns floating in the dark. When he sat her down, his hands rose to her face, and Luke cupped her cheeks like she might vanish if he didn't hold her steady. She looked into his bright eyes as his thumbs wiped her tears away.

"This is where I belong," Luke whispered, voice shaking. "I can make my life here. With you. If that's what you want, too."

Mariah couldn't find the words so she nodded over and over, her smile turning into a laugh so full of joy she imagined the creatures in the wilderness around her stopping to listen.

Wiping away tears, she finally stopped laughing. She stood on her tiptoes, looking deep into Luke's eyes.

"I don't want to be afraid anymore."

"Neither do I." His voice was barely above a whisper.

And slowly, Mariah kissed him, knowing that the longing inside her she'd felt for so long would be gone when she awoke, replaced with the splendor of a new beginning.

Epilogue

Three months later

The gift shop at Twin Pines Lodge smelled like pine-scented candles, new T-shirts, and peanut butter fudge.

The lodge had just been inundated with its afternoon rush, but for a rare five-minute stretch, the shop was quiet. Luke took the opportunity to straighten a stack of trail maps and turn around a ceramic mug so the park logo faced forward. Mariah would laugh if she saw how obsessively he organized this place.

The truth was, he liked it. The creaky floorboards, the humming overhead fan, the kids pressing sticky hands against the display case while begging their parents for candy or plush toys. He liked the conversations with customers and the quiet stretches when he could look out the windows and see the sun flashing on the lake.

It wasn't just a job. It was a life. One he had chosen, fully and deliberately.

Footsteps clicked across the floor behind him, followed by a familiar voice.

"You know that mug won't sell any faster just because you turned it around like that."

Luke grinned and turned around to find Mariah leaning against the doorframe, her hair pulled back in a ponytail, the lodge's hunter green polo matching his.

"Maybe not. But they look better. Come here."

She stepped forward and he wrapped his arms around her waist, tugging her close. They swayed a little in the quiet of the shop.

"Slow day?" she asked, resting her chin on his shoulder.

"For now. I think families wanted to get to their cabins and unload before the storm hits."

"Good. That means you can take your break."

He pulled back to look at her, brushing a loose strand of hair behind her ear. "You're awfully persuasive, you know that?"

Mariah smiled, eyes soft. "I just know a good thing when I see it."

Luke kissed her, gently and quickly, as the bell above the gift shop door chimed and a family spilled inside. But even as they stepped apart, their fingers stayed linked, and Luke knew this:

He hadn't just changed his address.

He'd found home.

Stay in touch

Thank you so much for reading! I truly hope you enjoyed this book. **Please take thirty seconds to leave a star rating on Amazon.** This is the best way to support independent authors.

If you'd like to stay in touch, sign up for **the Enchanted Mountains newsletter** at eleanorromanybooks.com to learn about new releases and upcoming events and to get subscriber-only extras!

Best,
Eleanor

About the author

Eleanor Romany is a romance author who believes in starlit kisses, long hikes through the woods, and the power of a good love story.

The ENCHANTED MOUNTAINS series is a love letter to Allegany State Park (ASP) in Western New York, the place where she, her husband, and his family vacation each summer. For the past 70 years, her husband's family has spent a week each summer at ASP, biking, swimming, fishing, kayaking, and hiking through its majestic landscape.

It's also the place where, deep in the forest along Eastwood Meadows Hiking Trail, her husband asked her to marry him, and she said yes.

When Eleanor isn't writing sweet, feel-good novellas set in the Enchanted Mountains, she's reading, checking out new restaurants, or daydreaming about her next fictional couple. She writes from somewhere cozy and quiet, and she always roots for happy endings.

For more information, visit eleanorromanybooks.com and follow her on Instagram at @eleanorromanywrites.

About the series

The ENCHANTED MOUNTAINS series from Eleanor Romany is a heartwarming collection of stand-alone romances set in the scenic beauty of fictional Twin Pines State Park.

While the heart of the series is the majesty of nature, the true stories are to be found within the characters. The books follow the lives of the people who come to the park all year long seeking peace, adventure, or escape and those who make up the Twin Pines community looking for the same things.

From chance encounters and second chances to late-night walks under starlit skies, love always finds a way in the Enchanted Mountains.

www.ingramcontent.com/pod-product-compliance
Lightning Source LLC
Chambersburg PA
CBHW062223150726
47991CB00006B/2409